BOUNCE

BECCA SEYMOUR

RAINBOW TREE PUBLISHING

For information, contact the author:
authorbeccaseymour@gmail.com

Editing: Hot Tree Editing

Cover Designer: BookSmith Design

Publisher: Rainbow Tree Publishing

E-book ISBN: 978-1-922359-72-8

Paperback ISBN: 978-1-922359-73-5

"I understand your pain. Trust me, I do. I've seen people go from the darkest moments in their lives to living a happy, fulfilling life. You can do it too. I believe in you. You are not a burden. You will NEVER BE a burden."

— Sophie Turner

"IT'LL BE FUN, THEY SAID. YOU'LL FEEL GOOD, THEY said. By the end of the day, you'll be lucky to be alive, said no bloody one." I wheezed out each word between heavy pants of breath. But it was no good. I had to stop before I collapsed and my red face finally caught fire and lit up the whole damn gorge.

A few steps ahead of me, Pete stopped and took in our surroundings. "Come on, Riley. There's a spot just around the curve of this trail where we're stopping for lunch."

I paused, grateful for the short reprieve, and eyed him suspiciously. "You said that an hour ago."

The arsewipe grinned. "This time I'm not lying."

I heard movement behind me and angled back.

Another cluster from our group came up from behind, which made me feel marginally better. I wasn't the last. "Fine, but I swear, if you're jacking me around, I'm dumping your swag in the river."

Pete snorted before turning back to the narrow dirt path and trekking on. Reluctantly I followed, knowing I had little choice but to finish the circuit. I had no idea how far we'd walked of the eighteen-kilometre route, but that last incline almost did me in.

Attempting to regulate my breathing, I focussed on the inhale and the exhale. *I can do this.* I really hoped so anyway.

It had taken Pete, one of my workmates, at least nine months to talk me into finally joining the group for a trial weekend. He'd promised me it was the perfect place for beginners, and while he hadn't said the words "especially if you're unfit," I knew that was pretty much the implication. But hell, if this was easy, I really was in worse shape than I thought.

As we reached the bend in the pathway, I closed my eyes briefly and sent up a silent prayer to whoever was looking down at me. All I needed was fifteen minutes, or maybe an hour—actually, half a day would be even better—to regroup and carry on. Once around the rock wall, relief caressed me.

About fifteen guys were spread out on the flattened area of grass next to a small creek, with some of the group perched on large rocks. Most of the men wore tees sporting the Outback Boys logo, Pete included. His was red and clung to his fit body well. The jury was still out about whether I'd be joining at this point. My main mission at the moment was surviving this bloody hike.

"Here's us." Pete stopped next to two other guys, both already chomping on sandwiches. "Mark, Trey, this is Riley." Pete indicated to me as I dropped my backpack and grunted in relief as my butt hit the hard ground.

"Mark." The man with dark hair and black-rimmed glasses stuck his hand out for me to shake.

"Hey." I managed a smile and gripped his hand before turning my attention to the man at his side. "Trey?"

His hand pumped mine a couple of times, a shy smile on his face. "Yep. Hi." Trey pulled back and looked me over. "You have water?"

I nodded and dragged my bag onto my lap to retrieve it. "Yes, thanks. I look like I need it that much, huh?"

Trey laughed, which lightened his features a little and made him appear more at ease with me crashing their space. "I remember what my first trek was like. Mark here took pity on me and had to all but drag me around the last few kilometres. I thought I was going to keel over and die." He cast a fond gaze at Mark, who leaned towards him and placed a tender kiss on his mouth.

"You did great. Now look at you," Mark said to Trey. "Speeding on ahead and giving even hardened adventurers a run for their money." He turned his attention to me. "Honestly, just get through today, and you'll find you'll love it. Doesn't mean you won't feel the burn tomorrow, though." He grinned.

A low groan tumbled from me. "Is it going to be that bad?"

Mark laughed good-naturedly. "Tomorrow we're kayaking, so at least your legs will be given a break. You'll be fine."

I hoped he was right.

"Great job, everyone." I turned my attention to a new voice. A guy called Frank had done a small greet and intro when we'd set up camp this morning. The tall, brown-haired guy currently holding my attention was most definitely not Frank—a smiley guy in his sixties. Nope. The hunk of deliciousness was perhaps close to my age and had such sculptured, toned legs that I doubted the measly eighteen kilometres from today would be felt. "My name's Aiden, for those first-timers." He glanced around, his eyes connecting with mine, a friendly smile forming on his lips.

Hot damn.

I gulped, impressed I remembered how to complete that simple action since my whole body reacted to the man.

"We'll stop for twenty minutes, then continue the trail." He looked at his watch. "We should be able to take another pit stop when we're on the last leg and be back at camp by five."

Frank walked to his side, saying, "Don't forget to holler if you need anything, and we'll let you know tonight about the plans for tomorrow." He turned to Aiden, who said something and laughed. While I couldn't hear the words, his laughter was deep and loud. Goosebumps travelled up my skin at the sound.

An elbow in my side had me whipping my head around. My gaze landed on Pete's shit-eating grin. "Pick your jaw up off the ground." While he spoke a little lower than usual, Mark and Trey snorted, clearly having heard him.

Heat flushed up my neck, spreading across my

cheeks. I cleared my throat and narrowed my eyes at Pete. "I was only paying attention."

"Uh-huh." Pete nodded, amusement dancing in his eyes. "And the drool?"

I huffed and shook my head. "Piss off."

"Aiden can't help being so easy on the eyes," Mark said. Trey nodded along with him. "I think it's one of the rites of passage for newbies in this group to get a hard-on for him."

My eyes widened. I didn't know these guys, had said a handful of words to them, so chatting about hard-ons didn't seem quite right. Not that I was a prude, but sex talk with strangers, or even friends, truth be told, wasn't exactly my thing.

"It's true," Pete confirmed. "Not only is he a good guy and doable, but he also has this whole elusive thing going on for him." There was a hint of wistfulness that had me peering over at Pete as he spoke. "Truth, I spent six months drooling over him, only to discover he wasn't interested."

"Is he with someone?" I asked.

It was Trey's quiet clearing of his throat that had me looking his way. "Erm," his voice dropped low, "no, but he was for a long time. James, his partner, died a while back."

My stomach hollowed out at the thought. I knew

all too well how loss could impact you. "That's tragic." I shook my head and cast a quick glance in Aiden's direction. He sat on a large rock by himself, eating his lunch and looking out at the impressive vista.

Mark spoke next. "Nobody here ever met him, I don't think. It was before Aiden moved to the Sunny Coast and joined our chapter. I'm not sure what happened exactly. But I can't even imagine how difficult it must be for him." Trey reached over and placed his hand on Mark's knee, and a sad smile pulled at my lips.

If that was the reason why Aiden didn't respond to advances, I got it completely.

"You want one?" Pete drew me out of my musings when he offered me a small chocolate bar.

I shook my head. "No, thanks." When Pete had finally worn me down to give this social-slash-activity group a try, it was with the premise of meeting new people and expanding my horizons a little. He was virtually the only person I spoke to in the office. He knew I didn't get out much. Home was originally in Perth, in a completely different state and a long way from the Sunshine Coast where I now lived. What had also made me change my mind was I'd put on a few kilos—admittedly, close to fifteen—in the last year, and I'd decided it was time to take better care of myself.

I had no grand plans to drop sizes or bulk up with muscles, but simple things like climbing four flights of stairs without needing a break and not being out of breath would be stellar.

Not that I was totally at ease with my weight gain.

But I wasn't especially bothered about my appearance. I didn't hit the clubs—not that there were many in the area beyond a monthly LGBTQIA+ community event—didn't tap into Grindr, and I wasn't even sure I wanted to be hooking up with anyone. Permanently or for a fling.

"No worries. More for me." He shoved the whole bar in his mouth, his cheeks puffing out. Our small group laughed at his ridiculousness while I quietly patted myself on the back for saying no.

Before long, it was time to pack up and get going. I groaned as I clambered to my feet.

"All good here?"

I jumped at the closeness of Aiden's voice and turned his way. We were almost eye to eye, a pleasant rarity, with just a couple of inches or so difference. My six three was usually the form that stuck out in the crowd. "Erm, yes, thanks," I answered after a beat, realising his focus was on me and he was waiting for a response.

"Excellent." He thrust his hand out. "Aiden." On autopilot, I took it, aware once again that my skin was heating. His strong hand gripped mine, his palm large like my own. His skin was rough, so much more so than mine. Being a computer programmer didn't leave much time for hard yakka.

"Riley." I smiled, hoping it came out naturally and I didn't come off looking shifty, something my big sister, in her once-teasing way, had told me many years back. Once that seed had been planted, I'd done nothing but water the bloody thing. "Good to meet you." I finally released his hand and swallowed, trying to get a grip on my nerves.

Talking to a good-looking guy was a struggle at the best of times. Aiden, though, was so spectacular that it sent my pulse skyrocketing. I played with the leather band on my left wrist, trying to keep my cool.

"Hey, Aiden," Pete said, much to my relief. "This is the Riley from work I was telling you about."

I blanched at that and turned my gaze to Pete, who did nothing but grin at me.

"Oh yeah, right. I remember you mentioning him." Aiden returned his attention to me. "I'm pleased you finally joined us." He angled his head, indicating we should start walking. I could do that. One step in front of the other without tripping and looking like a jerk. "How'd you handle the first ten kilometres?"

"Really, is that what we've done?" Surprise flickered to life. Holy shit. I grinned, completely proud of myself.

"It sure is." Aiden offered me a friendly smile. "Did it feel like more or less?" I looked ahead as we walked side by side, the trail wider in this section. Mark and Trey were a few metres ahead, Pete a few steps behind them.

"Less, I think. Even though I'm already exhausted," I admitted with a shrug. "I can't remember the last walk I went on." Embarrassment had me flushing. I didn't want him to think I was lazy, though admittedly, outside of work, I holed up at home doing very little.

"Well, that's brilliant that you're taking it in your stride. Ten kilometres is no easy feat." I cast a glance at him as he continued. "Starting off is always hard, and there's always reasons not to do it, right?"

I nodded. "Yeah, but I think I finally realised they were excuses, you know?" My honest words just continued to tumble forth. "I'm thirty-six and creeping closer to the big four-oh." I snorted. "It was about time I got healthy, and this seemed like a good start.”

“It really is. And the last few kilometres will seem so easy compared to this morning.”

“You think?”

“Yup.”

“You’re trying to make me feel better, huh?” I gave a small laugh.

His smile widened. “Maybe.” He shrugged. “I only got back into fitness outside my regular day and all this adventure stuff a few years back. I remember the blisters and how much it sucked.”

“Hey, I didn’t sign up for blisters. Is there an Uber service around here or something?” I joked, enjoying how easy Aiden was to talk to. Perhaps it was the whole unattainable thing that had me loosening up, maybe that I understood the devastation of loss, but whatever it was, my steps came easier with him walking beside me, and our flowing conversation seemed natural.

“I think we’re just out of range for a rescue.”

We continued trekking through the gorge. The scent of the gums and ferns surrounded us, their aroma calming. This part of the trail seemed much easier than the first half of the journey. That the looped course was a steady gradient down eased the ache in both my feet and my butt.

After hiking in companionable silence for a while, Aiden asked, "Are you feeling good about kayaking tomorrow?"

I gave a one-shoulder shrug. "I suppose. Just wondering how long it'll take before I capsize the damn thing." My laugh was a little hollow. For real, I had a picture already in my head of squeezing myself in, only for it to wobble, tip, and turn me over in seconds.

When Aiden stopped without speaking, it took me a couple of beats to realise he was no longer by my side. As soon as I noticed, I paused and turned to face him. My brows dipped in concern. "You okay? Something wrong?" He looked fine. I snorted internally. "Fine" wasn't close to just how good Aiden looked.

His eyes appeared grey in this light, and I briefly wondered if they took on different shades depending on the time of day and where he was. "You'll do great tomorrow."

"O-kay." I dragged out the word.

He seemed to deliberate over something, but I had no idea what as he peered over at me for a few beats, gave me a firm nod, then indicated for us to continue.

Confusion rumbled deep in my gut, unsettling our easy walk. I focussed ahead, and Pete was nowhere in view. I'd been so caught up chatting with Aiden, I hadn't seen my friend march on ahead. At some point soon, we'd be making that pit stop Aiden mentioned earlier. Hopefully it wouldn't be long.

An awkward half hour later, we reached the rest of the group. Tension dripped from my shoulders when I spotted Pete. His gaze was fixed on me, a grin on his mouth. I peered over at Aiden before saying, "Thanks for keeping me company." My lips pulled up, forming a smile I didn't quite feel. It was odd as hell. The mention of kayaking, along with Aiden's bizarre reaction, had thrown me for a loop. I needed to escape so I could breathe again. "I best go and make sure Pete's not doing something crazy. You know what he's like." Or I assumed he did. Pete was a riot, a bit of a PITA, as well as a good guy. But he was also known for stirring up trouble and causing mayhem every now and then. He was a great excuse to get away. "I'll catch you later."

I turned to head towards Pete, only to catch my foot and stumble. I felt myself tumbling forwards, slow motion beginning to play out as I tried to move my hands to protect my face. Not even halfway down, I jerked abruptly, coming to a stop.

"Whoa there." Aiden's firm hands were on me, one arm wrapped around my chest. "You okay?"

Wide-eyed, I nodded, angling to face him. With Aiden wrapped around me, it was impossible not to see the green flecks in his grey eyes. "Yeah, thanks."

He shifted, helping me get myself upright. With my face on fire, I was eager to escape, to hide behind Pete or perhaps jump in the river I could hear in the distance.

"I can be such a klutz." I forced humour into my words, trying to overcome my mortification. "My parents used to legit carry a first aid kit with them everywhere we went, even if just to the supermarket as a kid. I once broke my little finger playing hopscotch." My eyes swept over Aiden's face, still so close his breath brushed against my skin. "Yeah, I know. Hopscotch. How's that even possible, right?" I seriously needed to stop talking, else I'd end up telling him how I got circumcised after a devastating encounter with a zipper.

That thought had me stepping out of Aiden's grasp. "Thank you," I managed again. "For preventing me from bouncing on my arse or my face." I turned abruptly, giving an awkward over-the-shoulder wave while trying not to spend too much time contemplating how strong Aiden must really be to prevent my backside from meeting dirt.

One thing I could be sure of, between him being untouchable and me being my usual charming, awkward self, it wouldn't take long for Aiden to forget this encounter as well as my name.

Chapter Two

AIDEN

RILEY. I WAS ABSOLUTELY TRANSFIXED BY EVERYTHING about this guy. From his messy hair that flicked up in odd ways on his right, to the dimple in his left cheek —for real, a dimple—to his fascinating awkwardness and chattiness. As soon as my gaze had collided with his during lunch, I'd felt it bone-deep that I needed to get to know this man.

That feeling, sense of need to connect, had happened only a handful of times in my life. The first was with Lee when I was six and playing soccer in the park. Thirty-two years later, he was still one of my best friends, despite the distance. The other was with Geffen and Mel, a couple I'd met in NOLA a good few years back when on holiday with James. According to Mel, if we didn't FaceTime at least once a fortnight to vent and shoot the shit, the world would end. There was no way I would argue with them, so the chats went ahead without fail.

After that, there was Timmy. He was a sort of given since he was my tearaway nephew, but as soon I'd held him in the delivery room, the bond was there. Then, of course, there was James. My heart still seared at the thought of him, at what I'd lost. But some memories were getting easier to laugh and smile over.

And now Riley.

And I had zero idea what to do with that.

With no other choice but to stand back and watch, I let him walk towards a grinning Pete. The last leg of the hike had been awkward. He'd kept his eyes forwards, fingers fiddling with the leather bands on his wrists. I hadn't pegged him for a guy who wore bracelets, and I liked that something so small had both surprised me and caught my interest. The leather on his wrists looked kinda adorable and a bit hippy on him, despite his casual clothing. But the awkwardness had been entirely my fault because of my weird reaction to him being down on himself. I hadn't liked it one bit. Somehow I'd found—in the last part of my functioning brain—the ability to shut the hell up and leave him be. Knowing the guy for under a handful of hours didn't exactly give me the right to challenge him on his self-perception. If anyone had attempted to do so to me, I wouldn't have hesitated in telling them to rack off.

"All good here?" Frank appeared by my side, his expression filled with uncertainty. I understood the reason why. While I was friendly and chatty when helping to manage and lead the activities we ran, it was rare I attached myself to anyone for so long.

"Yeah." I dragged my gaze away from Riley, who was sitting down close to Pete. The pair appeared deep in discussion, and I couldn't help but wonder if there was something more between them. "All good. You want to finalise the details for tomorrow now or tonight?"

Frank paused for a beat, his concerned gaze roaming my face. "Sure. We can now if you want. It'll give us more time to relax later on."

I nodded, relieved with the focussed conversation. After taking a swig of my drink, I asked, "Have you let Bruce know the new numbers?" Bruce was from the local hire place that'd be fitting our group up with kayaks and life jackets.

"Yeah. He's expecting us at eight thirty, so we'll need to leave by seven thirty."

This group trip was for two nights due to the

public holiday. We'd arrived early this Saturday morning to set up before starting our day of gentle hiking and would be leaving after some rock climbing on Monday.

That was my favourite part of this trip. There was nothing like the burn of climbing and launching between holds to get my adrenalin pumping.

"Have you decided where we'll stop for lunch?"

Frank bobbed his head. "I was thinking the bank just past the singed gum." I knew exactly where he meant. There was a great place to bank and eat not too far from a huge-arse gum tree. It had all but burst in a storm when hit by lightning years back. It had been before my time, but the partially destroyed gum was still there and looked kinda cool.

"Sounds good."

"So what do you think of the new recruits?"

I fought hard not to glance in Riley's direction. "They all seem like good guys."

"Mick and Tony seem like a nice couple."

They did. I'd chatted to them briefly at the beginning of the day when we'd set up camp. It was good to have a mix of people in the group, so having another couple helped to balance our existing group of nineteen out a little. It prevented our outdoor activity group from being about hooking up. Not that there was anything wrong with that, and not that it didn't happen a few times. When I was still in Alice Springs and first checked out the nationwide group, it was because it was focussed on getting together to simply enjoy physical activities while adventuring.

There was no real hierarchy, no competition, just guys from different walks of life wanting a break from the grind while building connections.

More recently, it was about getting out of my head and heartache and trying to get a life.

"And how about Riley?"

I controlled my reaction, all too aware Frank knew something was up. "What do you mean?" Playing coy was not my usual reaction to a situation, but being evasive seemed like the best response with my brain so muddled.

Frank quirked a silver-streaked eyebrow at me. "You just spent the last couple of hours with him, right?"

"Yeah, right." I nodded. "He was easy to talk to." I planned to leave it there, but Frank, it seemed, had other ideas.

"Very different to Pete."

My brows dipped low, wondering what he was implying.

"Just not the type of guy I expected Pete to be friendly with, is all."

My gut tightened, and unease settled in my chest. It was unlike Frank to be bitchy, if that's what he was being. Was he suggesting— I stopped there, not allowing myself to get worked up over Frank's words.

"Right." Perhaps I should have asked him to explain, to speak clearly, but with Frank being on my case the past twelve months or so about me branching out and dating, there was no chance I'd give him ammunition.

I didn't even know if I was attracted to Riley. He was cute, which seemed ridiculous as he was a bigger guy than me. But there was still something about him that pulled at me.

"It's about time, right?" A quick glance at my watch told me we still had a few minutes, but some of the clusters were already shifting and packing up. "I can take the lead on this one if you want to follow up."

"Sure." Frank nodded, appearing a little perplexed. That was fine by me. Much better than having a conversation I didn't want to have.

It didn't take much longer before we were back on track and closing in on the campsite. We weren't roughing it on this trip. It was why we promoted it as an ideal trip for people new to the group.

There were flushing toilets, showers, and free barbeques around, and thankfully not a long drop in sight.

With no strict timetable once we got back to the camp, members were free to spend the time however they wished. But we still organised a big cookout for those who wanted to join us at seven. After that, we usually got a campfire going as long as there wasn't a fire ban in place.

I'd brought my guitar with me, and I knew a few others had too.

After dumping my pack in my tent, I wrestled off my hiking boots and pulled out my thongs to shove on my feet. I needed a shower to unwind and wipe off the sweat and confusion of the day.

In no time at all, I stood beneath the lukewarm water. I was relieved I'd managed to catch a shower before the heat ran out completely. Lathering myself up, I focussed on making my shower as quick as possible, sure others would be wanting to rinse off. I heard all three other showers going and expected there'd be a queue.

Satisfied I was cleansed of grime, I knocked off the tap and wrapped my towel around my waist. I planned to dress and dry in the small communal changing area to release the shower cubicle for someone else.

Mark was waiting.

"Oh, hey. It's all yours. I even left you some heat."

"Brilliant." He smiled at me. "Last time it was bloody freezing. Learnt my lesson after that."

I laughed. Mark was a nice guy, and he and his husband were one of the first couples I met when I relocated. "You joining the main camp for dinner tonight?" I asked as I strolled past him.

"Sure am. We'll be there."

I nodded and moved around the small wall partitioning off the changing area. Foot frozen in place, I wobbled a little, unsure of my next move. Riley was in the small space by himself. A towel was on his head, and he was rubbing his hair. At the moment, he hadn't seen me.

"Hey, Aiden, you already showered?"

I winced at Frank's voice. Surely it was obvious with water still trickling off me.

"Yeah, thanks." I didn't look behind me, but my eyes immediately connected with Riley's when he pulled the towel away and stared back at me, looking like a deer caught in headlights. "Hey." I stepped further into the changing area, my chance to do a runner long over. I glanced around the small space. With two of the benches covered with items, I had little choice but to take the spot next to him.

Discomfort settled in me when I stopped by his side, with what I was sure was an awkward smile on my face. He'd taken up finishing off rubbing his hair, but he'd turned away from me, his expanse of back on display. A large, jagged scar about fifteen centimetres long curved across his back and waist. I tore my gaze away. I should not be eyeing up Riley. Hating the awkward silence that had settled, I swallowed before asking, "How are you feeling after today? All good?"

His brown eyes darted to mine. "Yeah, thanks." He gave a small shrug. "Sure I'll feel it tomorrow, though, which is a good thing, right?"

I relaxed a little. "Sure is. It'll just keep on getting easier."

"Maybe." He gave a little shrug.

I offered him a smile. "It definitely will if you keep attending. You'll soon find your stride and be wondering what you spent your previous weekends doing."

"You think?"

"I know." My gaze flicked down to his bare chest for the briefest of moments, but long enough for him to recognise I was checking him out. Hell, I was honest to God flirting. I thought I'd forgotten how since it had been so long.

"So...." Riley cleared his throat.

When he didn't continue, I realised what the problem was. His hair had been towel-dried, and he needed to dry off and dress. I swallowed at the thought of seeing him buck naked and mentally shook myself. I was not an inappropriate dick. While in the past there'd been plenty of guys dropping their towels almost as soon as I'd entered the communal area in the hope of me checking them out and us both getting lucky, it was crystal clear that's not what Riley was about.

"So, yeah," I said as I angled away from him, eyes fixed on the wall, "are you eating at the main camp tonight?" I dried myself down, my rubs efficient and focussed.

He didn't answer straight away, but I was determined not to look at him so he had some semblance of privacy. After a beat, there was movement and the sound of fabric before he said, "Yeah, I think that's what Pete said."

I pulled on a pair of shorts and dumped my damp towel on the side. "Great. Most of the group do, but there's no drama if you choose to stay close to your tent."

I risked a glance in his direction just as he pulled up his own shorts. My tongue stuck to the roof of my mouth. He was going commando. With that visual bobbing around in my head, I jerked my gaze away quickly.

"Then you have a fire or something, right?" Riley asked. In my peripheral vision, I saw him angle towards me, so I safely did the same. A light pink covered his cheeks, but his eye contact was strong.

"Yeah," I answered with a smile. "The recent lifting of the fire ban has been a relief." The dry winter had been difficult and dangerous for far too many Aussies impacted by a harrowing number of bushfires. The last six weeks of steady rain rolling in had made life so much easier. "I have my guitar," I continued. "I can't sing for shit, but I can play. We usually have marshmallows and a few drinks."

"I don't drink. Alcohol, that is."

My heart stuttered at that. "Me neither." My lips lifted slightly as I wondered what other discoveries there were to make about this man. Yeah, a lot, obviously. A few hours of conversation weren't enough to honestly know someone, but the desire to get to know him better remained. If anything, it burned even brighter.

"Oh." The pink turned to red on his skin as he smiled. He looked away and picked up his T-shirt. "That's good."

As he tugged his tee over his head, I took my fill as quickly as possible. A dark smattering of hair covered his chest. A smooth, softer stomach led to his shorts that hung low on his hips. The expanse of skin caught my attention for too long, making me consider what it would taste like, feel like under my touch. Wide-eyed at the direction of my thoughts, I grabbed my own T-shirt and tugged it on, using the process to get myself together.

Lust, it seemed, was what was driving me towards getting to know Riley better. Unexpectedly, a bubble of excitement at the prospect grew inside me.

"So I'll catch you later then?"

His voice had me looking his way as I pushed my arms through the sleeves. "Yeah, sure." I smiled and gave him a chin lift as he collected his shower stuff and hightailed it out of there.

As soon as he was gone, I exhaled, turned, and sat down, head dipping low and falling on my hands.

"Don't worry, it wasn't that bad," Frank said quietly, causing me to both jump and groan. I finally looked in his direction and was met by a wide smile. "Honestly, your flirting is a little rusty." He paused a moment, brows lifting. "That was what you were attempting, right?"

I snorted. "I think so, yeah, maybe."

Frank laughed, stepping fully into the area, already showered and dressed. "That's a relief. There was this whole awkward, almost adorable thing going on between you. It was a bit like watching... I don't know, a foal trying to walk for the first time. Clumsy and wobbly, but cute."

"Nope." I shook my head despite my laughter. "I can't...." I groaned again before saying, "Was it really that bad?" My voice remained low.

"Not so bad that a bit of practice won't fix it."

I exhaled, collected my belongings, and stood. Reality then hit me. "Please don't say anything to anyone." I was a private guy, and the thought of any more gossip surrounding me made my stomach dip.

"My lips are sealed." He jerked his head towards the exit. "Come on. Let's get settled and the barbie going."

Relieved he was giving me an out, I followed Frank to where we'd set up. On the way, he said quietly, "I won't say anything else, but it's good to see you excited about meeting someone."

There went my stomach again. Losing James was the hardest time in my life. At one point, I thought it had broken me. And to be showing interest in someone else was new—the feeling alien but not wholly unpleasant. "Thanks," I mumbled, appreciating his kindness.

He nodded and fell silent as we parted ways so I could take my wash bag to my tent and collect what I needed to eat.

***

I SIGHED IN CONTENTMENT WITH A FULL STOMACH AND eased down in the small camp chair that was super comfy despite its rough appearance. I glanced around the campfire Frank had set up in the fire pit, noting most of the group was here. My gaze lingered on Riley, who was standing next to Pete, Mark, and Trey. Pete seemed to be holding court, using his hands animatedly, making the other three men laugh.

A spark of annoyance pounced at me, frustrated he was making Riley laugh, and more to the point, keeping Riley away from the main gathering around the flames.

Frank's presence at my side had me pulling my focus away.

"Water?" he asked, handing me an unopened bottle.

"Yeah, thanks." I took it from him, doggedly avoiding recasting my attention back to Riley.

"You know, it's okay to get off your arse and go and join them, say hi, right?"

I stiffened a moment, pissed off he could read me so well. There was no point denying my reaction. That was for sure. "I'm good here." Truth was, it felt somewhat inappropriate to be all but hounding Riley for his time. From the very little I knew of him, he didn't seem like he was here for a hook-up. And neither was I. But when his laughter reached my ears again, I couldn't help but mull that last thought over.

A hook-up wouldn't be so inappropriate, right?

"In that case, play something and stop ogling the man." He snorted, and my lips twitched. Few people called me on my shit these days, but Frank was definitely one of them.

"Fine." I leaned over, balancing precariously in my canvas chair, as I reached for my case. Latching on, I tugged it towards me and took out my acoustic guitar. I had a couple more at home, decent ones. This one did the trick but was the only one I brought with me when travelling and camping.

I strummed a little, mulling over what to play. Looking out over the fire in the direction of the just visible river, I allowed my fingers to catch on an easy melody. It was a sweet piece I'd created myself a couple of years ago. It was effortless and calming, so much so, I eased into playing while allowing my gaze to become unfocussed.

The temperature had cooled nicely, and there was a gentle breeze barely putting a nip in the air. It was a perfect night for camping; I considered tonight I may actually sleep in my swag under the stars rather than under the cover of my small tent.

I shifted my focus with my fingers working the strings, noticing a few of the guys had dropped their conversations. I assumed so they could listen to the music.

Then the sound of a second guitar had me smiling. I grinned over at Cameron. He'd heard me play this often enough that he'd learned how to fit in effortlessly.

Movement had me angling a look to my right. My eyes connected with Riley's. His focus was intent, apparent even in the dark—the flickering flames and the few camp lights dotting the area the only source of light.

Unwilling to look away, I softened my gaze, trying not to stare too attentively. A small smile lifted my mouth, a gentle request for him to relax, and admittedly, I wished it was inviting enough for Riley to head on over.

Pleased he didn't look away and break the connection, I harnessed my courage and gave a small head tilt to my side where I knew an empty space was. He flicked his attention in that direction. His eyes widened a fraction, and I flicked my gaze to Pete, who was behind him as he whispered something to Riley.

With Riley's eyes back on mine, he mumbled something to Pete and gave a small nod. A moment later, I grinned widely as Riley headed towards me, stepping around a couple of guys before clasping what I assumed was the chair and pulling it next to me.

Once he was by my side, I chanced a smile at him. When his lips tilted up as he looked at me, I exhaled and concentrated on my strings, changing the song into a different tune.

"Oh, nice one. I haven't heard this one for ages,"

Cameron said. He kept up. Trying desperately not to cut off the song early merely so I could stop and talk to Riley, I focussed on the rhythm and then sang the words in my head, not willing to do so aloud.

Now is not the time to flee
Forgetting me is not the end
It doesn't have to be to find someone anew
'Cause, baby, we both know he's more than a friend.

I considered the words, wondering how to handle Riley and my desire to get to know him better.

Finally, I finished the song and placed the guitar down. A few guys applauded, Riley included, and I turned my attention to him.

"That was amazing."

"Thanks," I said, my lips curving high.

He cast a quick look at Cameron when he started playing an old 90s tune and Sammy and John sang along. "He's good."

"Yeah," I agreed.

"But I think you're better."

That got my eyes fixed firmly on his face and his heating cheeks, obvious even under the glow of the fire. My stomach somersaulted at his sweetness.

"Don't let Cameron hear you say that," I whispered. "He's a great guy, but his ego can't handle my awesomeness."

Riley laughed, and I mentally high-fived myself. His laugh had a deep and surprising gruffness. He was a tall man with wide-set shoulders. There was nothing especially delicate about his features. They were masculine, and if I hadn't already spent a few hours talking to him, on appearances alone, I would have said he was rugged. Which he definitely was. But throw in his gentle manner, which seemed at odds with his bigger frame, and Riley was a conundrum I was keen to discover more about.

"How are you feeling after today's walk?" I asked, grasping for any thread to make easy conversation and not quite convinced I hadn't already asked him this same question.

He shifted a little in the canvas chair, looking a bit uncomfortable as he did so. "Tired, but good at the moment." He shifted again.

"You all right there?" I gave a chin lift to his seat.

"Err, yeah." He gave a quiet snort. "Just not used to sitting so low or having my knees by my chin." As soon as the words were out of his mouth, he clamped his mouth shut. Meanwhile, I pressed my lips together, trying my hardest to get the image of him in that position out of my head. "I mean, you know, long legs."

I grinned. It would have been too easy to go with innuendoes, but everything about Riley screamed for me to leave it alone, so I did, offering an understanding smirk. "I get it." I kicked my own long legs out. "One of the drawbacks, right?"

Relief and something akin to gratitude passed over his features. "Yeah. Plus I'm not the most coordinated. It was enough to have the confidence to sit in this contraption." He looked down dubiously at the blue camping chair. "I've been avoiding the damn thing."

Pleasure rippled along my skin. "Well, I'm pleased you made the effort for me."

"Oh" escaped his mouth before he stopped. For a second, I thought he was going to argue. Instead, he surprised me with "Me too."

My satisfaction was instant. After a quick glance around the group, I saw Cameron still playing, and singing from others. Frank had disappeared from my side, and I noticed that we had privacy despite the size of our group. I took the opportunity to shift my chair around a little, angling myself towards him. At the movement, my eyes dropped down to his bobbing Adam's apple.

Despite being out of the game for so long, I was sure that Riley was just as curious about me. Why else would he have braved it to come over and sit by my side? He seemed to be out of his comfort zone in doing so, making his gesture even sweeter.

"So where is it you work? I know you said you live near Eumundi. Is it close to there?" I asked.

"Yeah, not too far away. The company I work for is a little off the beaten track, which is nice, not having to go into one of the busier towns or the city, especially when tourist season is going on."

"Isn't tourist season all the time in Eumundi?"

He laughed a little and nodded. "It feels like it sometimes." He tilted his head. "You live close by?"

I bobbed my head. "Yeah. I actually used to live in Eumundi a while back when I first moved from out west. I live out near Kilkivan, out on a property there."

His eyes widened in recognition. "Oh, wow. I didn't think this chapter... or group—"

"Chapter," I confirmed.

"—stretched that far. I thought it was just the Sunny Coast."

I shrugged. "The area north of Noosa is so rural and spread out, there weren't enough numbers to create a chapter of their own, I suppose." I quirked my brow at him. "Not many gay property owners, or out ones anyway, amongst the thousands of acres our council covers, you know?"

He laughed at that. "I can imagine." He went quiet, and I gave him a moment to digest. "So, you have cows?"

"You could say that." I offered a wry grin. "I have a couple thousand acres."

His eyes sprang wide, amusing me. Always a similar reaction from city folk. Or I assumed that was the case, based on what I'd learned about him so far.

"Holy crap. That's huge."

Well, I like to think so. I clamped down on the words once again, instead settling on, "I suppose. Not compared to those out west."

"So how many cows is that?"

"Just three hundred head at the moment. It's been a little dry. Things have finally calmed down, so we're breeding a few." I looked around the area, appreciating the lush grass under my feet and surrounding us. "Madness that it's only a couple of hours away and we're so much dryer."

"That must be tough."

"It can be," I agreed. While we were no longer in drought, I was a firm believer in not overstocking. I opened the lid of my bottle and went to take a swig. "Sorry." I stopped myself from drinking. "Do you need a drink?"

A smile lifted his mouth. "I'm good, thanks. I actually have one here." He angled to the side and leaned over.

I saw it happen but wasn't quick enough. His chair wobbled the barest of moments before giving up the fight and tipping over. Riley fell with a grunt as I jumped out of my chair.

He attempted to scramble up, but the chair was still attached to him. A couple of guys behind me chuckled, and while admittedly there were more times than not I'd laugh over a friend falling and being a klutz, I already knew from the change in atmosphere that Riley was not taking this in his stride.

"Hey, there." I reached his side and crouched. "Let me help you." His face was dark, cast in my shadow, but I saw enough in his eyes to know he was mortified. "Come on." I held on to the chair arm while holding my other hand out for him." For a moment, I didn't think he would grasp it, but my relief was quick when he finally made contact.

"Holy shit," Pete said, heading on over. "What happened? You okay?"

I squeezed Riley's hand and tugged, helping him up. "All good here," I hollered. "And all my fault." I shook my head and laughed. "Riley here saved my own arse when I went to fall."

Pete stood by our side, and Riley's face was downcast, though his hand remained in mine. I gave one more squeeze, hoping to reassure him. "Aren't you the regular hero, Riley?" Pete said with a laugh.

"Well, I'm not quite—"

"He is that." I interrupted. "Luckily for you and everyone else it means I'm not damaged, so I can push you to the limit tomorrow when kayaking."

Pete groaned in exaggeration, as did a few more in the group.

"Relaxing, chilled weekend get-together," Pete grumbled. "That's what I signed up for."

"I didn't read that on the agenda. How about you, Frank?" I called out, spotting him a little off to the side.

Frank's laugh was loud. "Heck no. Adventure beckons, which means there's no going easy."

As Pete turned away and I saw others return to their conversations, I gave my full attention to Riley. His head was up, his gaze steady as it connected with mine.

"You didn't have to—"

"I did." I shrugged a little, casting him a wink. "I should have just been a gentleman and passed you my water."

Pleasure shot through me when that pulled a smirk from him.

"Well, I appreciate it. Thank you."

"Anytime."

"Err, so maybe…" He looked down at our joined hands. I waited for him to release, and he did, all too quickly. I liked the softness of his skin. Liked that his hand was the same size as mine. "I think that's my cue to turn in for the night." He took a step away, putting a more acceptable distance between us.

"Yeah," I begrudgingly agreed. "Six thirty start in the morning."

"You're serious?" he said with a groan, effectively cutting the growing tension.

I laughed in response. "Afraid so. We get a lie-in."

"Only for those up with the—"

"—cows?"

His eyes lit up with amusement, the humour evident even in the flickering light. "Fair enough." He shook his head, his shoulders now fully relaxing. "I'll make a promise to never complain about my alarm getting me up at seven again."

"Wise words." I shot him a wink. "You're all okay with your tent? Set up okay?"

He nodded while he spoke. "I think so. It's been a long time since I camped out, but I used to a fair bit as a kid with my dad in Perth."

That's where the accent was from. "That's great. You'll soon become an old hat and perhaps be able to pick it up again maybe when your folks come...." His face dropped, and I quickly trailed off. "Shit, sorry." There was no way I'd continue down that line of questioning. "So, tent," I said. "I'm heading that way now, so I'll walk over with you."

He nodded, a little more subdued than a few moments ago. I could have punched myself. I knew better than most how seemingly innocent questions or conversations could lead the unaware down a shitty path.

"Let me grab my things."

He did the same, and we moved away, saying goodnight to the blokes that were still around, a few other guys trailing after us.

"This you?" I asked when he stopped outside a small tent.

"Yeah." He offered me a tentative smile, which I happily took, relieved he didn't appear to be as uptight. "Thanks again for the save."

I breathed deeply, my lips lifting. "Anytime." I nodded over to my own space about twenty metres or so away. "I'm over there, but I think I may grab my swag and head a few more metres away to get some quiet."

"Under the stars sounds nice," he said quietly. Before I could even think about how to respond, he lifted his hand in a sweet, somewhat awkward wave and took the steps needed to the entrance of his tent. "See you in the morning," he offered.

"Yeah, see you in the morning," I managed to say as he bent over and got on his knees to crawl inside. I quickly turned away from the image and considered heading for a cool shower before I attempted to sleep.

Chapter Three

I'd turned old overnight. For real. Hobbling like an old man, looking like I had something unpleasant shoved up my arse, was both painful and unpleasant as hell. I couldn't imagine I appeared particularly attractive either. I winced when that thought hit me. At the same time, I glanced up and my eyes landed on Aiden. A smile lit his face the moment our eyes met. Butterflies took flight in my stomach, taking me by surprise and making me stumble.

Yep, the grace of a gazelle right here in my size elevens.

My arms swivelling and a grunt escaping, I thanked all that was holy that I righted myself before I face-planted. As I angled up, heat filling my cheeks, I considered changing my route but knew there was no escape.

Wide-eyed, Aiden's gaze was intense and concerned. "Good save." His smile quickly followed as my lips curled upwards. How could they not when his grin was infectious and pointed at me?

"I have moments of recovering and saving face. It's something I have a talent for." It was easier to go with the flow and draw attention to my two left feet rather than submit and run.

"Gold medal material for sure." He angled his head towards the line of life jackets hanging up near the parked van. "You here to grab a jacket?"

I bobbed my head and grimaced a little in distaste. The thought of wearing a stinky jacket, let alone making sure I asked for the right size so I didn't look like a pig in a blanket, was not a task I looked forwards to.

His laughter drew my attention to him and away from the offending jackets. "Come on." He tilted his head, that same handsome smile on his face. "They're not that bad. Honest. I'll help you."

I somehow kept my groan inside, even more mortified that he'd have to see me squeeze into one, but what the heck was I supposed to do when he tapped me on the forearm and gestured for me to start walking?

Reluctantly, I travelled in the direction of the red and blue jackets, mumbling a half-hearted "Thanks."

Aiden cast a quick glance over me, seemed to make a decision, and reached for a red jacket. "This'll do perfectly." He undid the zip and held it open for me.

I immediately cast a surreptitious glance around the place, seeing a few others getting themselves kitted out, but not spotting anyone else receiving help. Not quite sure how to respond other than with a smile that I was sure looked more like a grimace, I stuck my arms in as quickly as possible and was prepared to zip myself up but startled at Aiden appearing before me.

"I've got it. These zips can be a pain in the arse. Once I got one trapped in my rashie and ended up having to cut the damn thing off."

I snorted, grateful for his effort to put me at ease. The distraction also helped, particularly with him in my space. It had been a long time since I'd had a gorgeous guy, especially one who spiked my interest, so close. In fact, the last time was so long ago, I'd have to pull out my iPhone 4 pre-Cloud to check the old calendar.

Which I legit still had. I had one of every generation, boxes and all. But that wasn't something I needed to be sharing with anyone, ever.

"Thanks," I eventually said, remembering I stood before the guy in silence while his hands were practically on me.

He zipped me up with practiced ease, then pulled away, looking happy with himself. "Perfect," he said.

"I feel like I should be rolled along or at least dipped in ketchup or something," I joked, feeling uncomfortable wrapped up so snugly.

Rather than laughter, a frown appeared between his brows. "It fits perfectly. The same size as me." The last words were said pointedly, the emphasis obvious.

Embarrassed by his defence and warm that he was trying to make me feel better, I blushed and glanced away. "So," I started, wanting to change the subject, "what's next?"

"Now's the fun part," he said, amusement back in his eyes. "We sit through a riveting thirty-minute safety talk and try not to fall asleep."

I chuckled, though sure he was right. Safety talks

were never known to be exciting, but if I was going to capsize—and the probability was high—then I needed to know how to not drown, and ideally not look like a dipstick while doing it. Because obviously, there was a non-dickish way to drown. I rolled my eyes internally and headed over to where the rest of the group was, surprised when Aiden kept step beside me.

I'd thought he was assisting everyone with the life jackets. The knowledge that he wasn't unfurled heat in my stomach. I side-eyed him, wondering if he'd direct us where to go as we edged closer to the group.

He did, leaving me with a smile when he whispered, "Quick, let's grab the bench while it's free. You'll fall over when you fall asleep otherwise."

I shot him an amused look as I followed after him and dumped my backpack on the ground, all too aware that the wooden bench wasn't exactly made for two men of our size. Our thighs brushed, our arms touched, and I had no desire to inch away —more than happy to lap up the reassuring press of this man's body against mine.

The whole time through the safety talk, I fought hard to keep my eyes focussed on the woman providing a range of instructions. Half-listening perhaps wasn't the best thing, especially given how accident-prone I legitimately was. Still, there was little chance my concentration could be wholly on anything as my body all but buzzed at my proximity to Aiden.

Although distracting, I relished in the awareness and admitted to myself I liked it. Even though I had no idea what to do about that.

As the woman wrapped up, my gaze drifted over to the left, landing on Pete. Surprise flittered in my chest when his eyes were already on me. I wasn't sure if he'd been looking my way for a while or it was by happenchance, but the look on his face was unreadable. Unusual for him.

Unsure if he was okay, I sent him a nod. Immediately, he quirked his brow before his eyes darted to my right, landing on Aiden before returning to me and then drifting away.

"Right," Aiden said, startling me.

Movement around the area alerted me to the talk being over and people getting ready.

"Right?" I responded, my uncertainty both noticeable and annoying. In an attempt to get my head back in the game, I stood, noticing the group making their way to the kayaks.

Standing before me, Aiden tilted his head. "You okay?"

"Yep. We doing this?"

His smile came quickly as he nodded.

A few steps away from the bench and closer to where it looked like we were collecting our kayaks, we paused as Pete stepped towards me. This time a grin sat on his lips, and he appeared more than okay.

"Do you want to grab number five, and I'll grab six?" Pete said, his attention solely on me.

I cast a gaze at the blue and red kayaks, noting their numbers. "Sure," I said.

"Actually," Aiden said, pulling my attention to him, his eyes on Pete rather than me. "I thought it'd make sense if I pair up with Riley."

Surprise of a different kind sped through me this time, and I stood a little straighter in awareness. I focussed on relaxing my expression, my gaze snapping to Pete when he said, "Why would it make sense for you to pair up with him?" There wasn't quite venom in his voice, but there was a hardness that took me by surprise. "Obviously we're pairing up since he's my friend and we came here together."

Confusion had me scrunching my brows. And there was no way I could ease that off my face. While he was absolutely right, his reaction didn't make a lick of sense. There was no issue with me pairing up with either man. Heck, I'd completely missed the part when the woman had provided that instruction, but this bizarre claim made me feel uncomfortable.

"Maybe I should just sit this activity out." The words slipped past my lips, and both men jerked their heads in my direction. "Wasn't there an odd number anyway?" I asked, defusing the awkwardness and more than happy to return to the campsite and play games on my phone.

"There's no chance of you missing out," Aiden said, his piercing eyes blazing in my direction. "You need to experience everything. It's why you came, right?"

I semi-reluctantly bobbed my head. He was right.

"You definitely can't miss out," Pete added, his tone sounding much more Pete-like. "It's taken me forever to get you here." He twisted his mouth after that, quite probably biting the tender flesh inside. He did that sometimes when he was thinking too hard. I'd worked with the guy long enough to pick up some of his nuances.

I huffed out a breath, saying, "Number five, you say?" to Pete.

With his eyes on mine, he nodded, that mouth of

his still gnawing and twisting away. A moment later, he straightened a little. "Aiden's probably right," he eventually said. It was casual sounding, but there was an unusual force behind it, as though him admitting it was an effort. "If you need help or struggle, he'll be able to help you better than I would." He looked over at Aiden without saying a word before he zipped up his jacket and met my eyes. "No drowning or shit, yeah? Everyone at work will kick my arse." He threw me a wink and spun around, heading away.

A frown creased my brow as I watched him go. Admittedly, Pete could be a peculiar guy at times, but that exchange was so random it hurt my brain.

Aiden startled me when he said, "I didn't mean to cause a rift or anything."

"What?" I turned in his direction quickly. "Who, Pete?" I scrunched my nose when Aiden nodded. "Nah, he's just being Pete," I said with a shrug. "He's sometimes like this. Either he's hyped up and the life of the party, usually being rude and crude, and generally really funny, but sometimes he'll do something that leaves me scratching my head." Though I didn't usually see him so serious, I thought to myself.

"If you're sure," he said. His concerned gaze roamed over mine.

The smallest of smiles curved my mouth when I nodded, saying, "I'm sure."

Not long after, I stared out at our surroundings in awe. The river was fairly fast-flowing from the recent rains, but not enough to have me crapping myself in fear. The breeze was gentle, though warm. I couldn't imagine being here any later in the year and doing this in the blistering heat. As it was, I had a mean sweat going, but I wasn't at the "dumped in water" stage. Though capsizing and swimming in the river sounded like a good plan too.

"Do you come to this gorge many times a year?" I asked Aiden as we paddled practically side by side.

"This will be the third and final trip here this year," he answered. "It's stunning, right?"

I nodded, taking in the landscape with the eucalypts standing tall and proud. "It is," I agreed. "Eumundi is beautiful, but there's something to be said for so much space and quiet." I angled to look at Aiden, his gaze already in my direction.

"It's why I love being on my property so much," he said, catching my attention. I was keen to discover as much about this man as possible. "The property stretches along the creek. When we've had rain, it's one of my favourite places to be. Nothing quite like it."

"You been there long?" I asked.

"Not really. I bought it about twenty months back. I moved my pops over with me when I headed east. He used to have a station out west, and this was the only way I could get him to retire, the grumpy old bugger he is," he said with a laugh.

I smiled. "You far out of town?" Was it bad I was eager to get phone reception so I could stalk his place on Google Maps? I suspected asking for coordinates wouldn't be appropriate, so I kept my mouth shut and waited for him to respond.

"About thirty minutes," he said.

"Is that a pain being so far out?"

His laughter disturbed the quiet, sending a couple of birds to the sky. "Thirty minutes isn't far," he said, continuing to laugh. "I spent years working out on my pops's station. Three hours to the closest spit of a town was far."

I grinned over at him, realizing I'd stopped paddling, too caught up in his laughter. Loud and deep, the sound had brushed over my skin, leaving goosebumps in its wake. "I suppose when you put it like that," I said sheepishly, "thirty minutes is nothing."

"But you'd know, right, from living all the way

over the west coast? Perth. There's bugger all there apart from the city."

It was rare I spoke about Perth. When I'd left, I'd wanted to rub the place from the map, try to cast away the memories I'd dragged away with me, ones that tainted me soul deep. But while I stiffened, just slightly, Aiden's presence calmed me, encouraged me to think about the place I used to call home.

"I was a city boy," I admitted. "It meant the last thing I was used to was space, but yeah, head away from the city and continue exploring Western Australia, and I think there's only a few places that can compete with that level of solitude or isolation."

"I figured you were a city boy," he said, beginning to paddle again, as we'd stilled for a few long beats.

I followed suit while saying, "You did, huh?"

"Oh yeah."

"Should I be insulted by that?" I quirked my brow over at him.

He laughed again, and I forced myself to keep on moving and not get sucked into his incredible laugh. "I'd prefer it if you weren't." A wink followed, and I snorted.

I lost his eyes as he looked ahead. "Looks like it's lunchtime." He indicated towards the area with a vast, lightning-struck tree that had me widening my eyes in awe. It was massive and strangely beautiful with its blackened limbs and split trunk.

"That went fast," I said, surprised. Though I didn't know how far we'd paddled, for it to be lunchtime already meant we'd clocked up a fair few kilometres.

"All the riveting conversation I provided," he said as his brows danced up and down.

"Yeah, that'll be it." My eye-roll was over the top and had the desired effect. His smile was wide, sending my pulse into overdrive.

His quirked brow was filled with a delightful sass that I didn't expect from him. There was so much to learn about this man. But with less than twenty-four hours before we parted ways, I had to wonder whether I should back away now to hold off the disappointment.

My eyes drifted down to the logo on his T-shirt.

Outback Boys.

Quite possibly, this could be the first of what I hoped to be many trips after all.

Chapter Four

I FLOATED IN THE WATER, A GRIN ON MY FACE, appreciating the coolness. The day had rushed on by too quickly, and I was well aware the reason for that was the man currently wading into the clear water.

"Holy shit, that's cold," Riley said, his eyes wide.

Laughter burst from me as I nodded. "Perfect, right?"

He didn't seem so convinced, but he continued deeper.

We weren't the only ones taking a dip. Most of us had decided a swim, or at least a paddle, was needed after a long day of kayaking.

After a few more steps, Riley eased himself down so he was sitting on the bottom, submerging to his chest. His blue T-shirt clung to him, and I had to wonder why he was still wearing it. The sun was still out, but we were in the shade. I supposed it gave the mozzies less skin to bite.

A gentle huff of breath escaped him, almost like a sigh. He sat with his arms behind him, face tilted to the sky, and I took a moment to drink him in.

He was a little soft around the edges for a big guy, not only tall but broad. It made him appear more approachable. There were smile lines around his eyes, and I appreciated the scruff on his jawline, wondering if that was just because of this weekend or if he always wore it that way.

He cricked his neck from side to side. The offer for me to rub his shoulders on the tip of my tongue almost escaped before I swallowed it back quickly.

Riley opened his eyes, his head angling in my direction. Rather than pulling my gaze away, I made eye contact with him, enjoying that he didn't flick his eyes away, so unlike his initial reaction just yesterday.

"You were right," he said. "It's perfect." He angled back, his legs floating up to the surface before dipping back under.

"A cold drink would go down nicely about now," I said, smiling.

Riley bobbed his head. "Yep, and then bed. I'm bloody knackered."

"You did really well today," I said. "It's no wonder you're tired. I think we all are." I cast a quick glance around to the group of us in the water. Most seemed spaced out and were murmuring. There was no crazy splashing, no wrestling, which was often the way when you threw a group of blokes together.

"And climbing tomorrow?" Riley asked. I returned my focus to him and smiled at his grimace. "That's both legs and arms for that one, right?"

I laughed when he shuddered. "You'll do fine."

He snorted. "Says you. Mr Super Fit."

My brows rose high. "I'm not that fit." Admittedly, I was in good shape. Between these adventures and working on the property, I was always active. I may have just thrown the half-hearted rebuke out there just to get his eyes on me.

And they were, immediately.

When he perused my body, a shot of heat jolted me. I wasn't naïve, nor did I have a giant ego, but it wasn't that rare when out with a group of gay or bi men to be eyed up. Most of the time, I ignored it. But not with Riley.

Between his shyness and awkwardness, mixed in with random moments of confidence and humour, he was fascinating. Yesterday, it was how he looked and his deep brown eyes that had initially caught my interest. But the more we spent time with each other, the more I hoped we could make an effort to get to know one another better.

Since James, there'd been no one else. Not a single man had sparked my interest. There was a whole heap of history that made it difficult for me to trust and move on, but I felt a connection for the first time. Taking a risk seemed like it might be worth it.

"So, do you think you'll stick with it?" I asked, gesturing around me, indicating the group.

"Perhaps ask me tomorrow, if I survive the climbing," Riley answered, his lips curling high.

"You'll be fine, but maybe I should find the paperwork and get you to sign up now, just in case." I trailed my fingers in the water as I spoke, only half serious about doing just that. "You seem like you've had fun," I continued.

Bobbing his head, he remained quiet a beat before saying, "I have. It's been different. Hard bloody work, which I suppose isn't a bad thing, but yeah, it's been good to do something active."

Splashing and movement to our side drew our attention. It was Pete. I shuttered my expression, still not quite sure about the strange interaction from earlier. If I had to guess, Pete was interested in Riley. But that didn't quite make sense either. I knew they worked together and had for a while. I also knew Pete flirted and had a laugh, and the couple of times I'd known him to hook up had been with men so different to Riley. Not that a man couldn't change his mind, but most guys I knew seemed to have a type, certainly from my observation of this activity group.

Pete's eyes were on Riley as he sat close next to him. Not close enough to touch, but I was still aware of their proximity. "Hey, Riley, how you holding up?"

"Knackered and looking forwards to bed," Riley answered, following up with a smile. "You okay? Have a good time?"

Pete nodded, eyes still on his friend. "Yeah, sore as hell. It's been a while since I was in a kayak. The current was a sod on the way back."

Unable to sit by and remain quiet, and honestly wanting as much of Riley's attention as possible before we parted ways tomorrow, I said, "It was. That wind picking up didn't help. Riley flew through it, though," I praised, gaze moving to Riley. His cheeks pinked, and my stomach somersaulted at his reaction. Once more, he cricked his neck. Whether it was because it was genuinely aching or he wanted to shake off his reaction, I was unsure, but when Pete's hand rose to Riley's neck, I froze.

"Bloody hell. Your neck's so damn tight." While Pete's voice remained steady with no inflection, there was no way in hell he wasn't flirting. And with the way Riley's eyes sprang open, his body tensing more, it didn't seem like they had the sort of friendship that involved them being touchy.

"Um, I'm good, thanks. A warm shower will help." When Riley flicked his gaze at me, his discomfort both surprised me and pissed me off.

"My bad," I said quickly. "I did promise to tell you when it was five thirty so you could get a head start on the showers. It's quarter to now." I stood swiftly, the water reaching my thighs.

Somehow, I held back my grin when Riley's gaze landed on my bare chest before moving to my groin, his cheeks turning from pink to red. When I flicked my attention to Pete, his usual jovial expression was wiped clean. There was no eye fucking in sight, unusual for the man. His eyes were hard while the rest of his expression seemed carefully neutral.

"You need a hand?" I asked Riley as I walked closer to him.

Wide-eyed, he gazed up at me, a position I could happily get used to. He shook his head. "I'm all good.

That shower's definitely calling, though." He stood. "I'll see you for dinner, Pete," he said, looking down at the man who remained in the water.

"Sure thing." Pete's response appeared light and friendly, and I watched as a smile formed on Riley's mouth.

Riley and I waded through the water, him slipping twice and me reaching out to hold him. After the second time, I simply held his hand, gripping him tightly, sure he'd be going down a third time. His face was aflame, but he held my hand, only grumbling at himself a couple of times about his inability to walk in a straight line.

I snorted when he called himself a dickhead. "You're not," I said with a grin. "I understand why you don't drink, though."

He glanced at me, just a few feet from the safety of the bank. "That's definitely one of the reasons for sure. Can you imagine all of this in a drunken stupor?" He grinned, and I was relieved he was finding the humour in the situation rather than being down on himself. "My sister used to say I had Shrek-like grace." His laughter was light. "She wasn't wrong." His smile remained as he shook his head, no doubt at something in his memory. "Between my poor coordination, my accident-prone feet, and apparently my ogre grace, I don't think I'm doing too badly, right?" When his smiling eyes moved to mine, I was captured by them, by his sweetness and gruffness.

My breath caught when I said honestly, "I think you're doing fucking brilliantly." His eyes widened, and I realised I hadn't held back from pushing heat into my words. There was a shift between us, and even more so than ten seconds earlier, I was more than aware of my hand in his. Knowing it was likely my intensity could freak him out, I said, "You know, Shrek was the hero all the way through those movies, right? I think it's safe to say you'll keep doing fine."

We reached dry land, and I reluctantly released his hand. For the first time I glanced around, taking in who was around. More than a couple of pairs of eyes were on us. Not usually behaving this way or interacting so close with anyone really beyond Frank, I expected I'd turned more than a few heads. One of many things I'd learned about myself over the years, though, was I didn't give a flying fuck what anyone thought of me.

Life was too short to be tied down to others' opinions or bull.

"Right, I'm going to go and sort stuff out for

tomorrow before grabbing a shower," I said, giving Riley the opportunity for some space. I'd dominated his time, so giving him breathing room wouldn't be a bad thing. "I'll catch you tonight."

"Sounds good," he said after a moment of quiet. A tentative smile touched his lips, and he angled away from me, heading back to the camp while I looked on, wondering if my intensity would have him running away.

***

WITH MY STOMACH SATISFIED, I SIGHED INTO MY canvas chair, pretty much mirroring last night. Eyes shut, it would be so easy to fall asleep, and I figured I'd definitely have an early night. I needed to make the most of it before I returned home tomorrow and life carried on as though this weekend had never happened.

While I was happy with my lot, I definitely didn't want to forget about meeting the sweet Riley. I opened my eyes and searched the darkness. The flames from the fire pit were high and bright, casting plenty of light and shadows. It didn't take long before I settled my gaze on the man who'd caught my attention.

He'd eaten with Pete, Mark, and Trey. And try as I might, the whole time my attention had drifted his way for the past hour at least. It meant I hadn't been the best company for Frank, whose partner couldn't make it this weekend, but he seemed content to lead the conversation.

"If you play again, he'll likely come on over, you know."

I cocked my head in Frank's direction as he spoke, having no doubt he was talking about Riley.

"You're like the gay pied piper." His loud snort followed, and my lips twitched at his absurdity. "You won't admit it, but pulling out that instrument..." He trailed off, his mouth twitching, and I waited for him to bite. He didn't, and I refused to. "Well, let's just say you've always had a fan club."

I rolled my eyes. "I wouldn't go that far."

"Uh-huh."

I shook my head at him. I wasn't blind or naïve. I'd been hit on plenty, but blatant wasn't my thing. If anything, it was a turn-off. Once more, my focus turned to Riley. A smile drifted across his lips at something Mark was saying, and while I liked that he seemed relaxed and happy, even with Pete, who sat at his side, a pang of envy jerked my awareness.

Was it wrong that I wanted to monopolise his time?

I didn't even bother considering the obvious answer to that thought.

Frank's sigh was loud and obnoxious, clearly intended to draw my attention.

"You're making me antsy. Just play your damn guitar already and get it over with."

My brows shot high when I looked at him. I didn't bother denying it as I asked, "Am I that bad?"

He nodded. "Yes, but not 'bad' necessarily, just clearly very interested and apparently not quite sure what to do about that." Sincerity shone in his eyes.

"You're right," I said quietly, deciding if I could attempt to confide in anyone, it may as well be him. Our friendship was solid, and while we didn't chat regularly or catch up socially, we stepped into our leadership-type roles here and spent most of our time with each other during our weekends away.

I also trusted him. And there were few of those in my life that I did.

"Do you think it's crazy if I ask for his number?"

His eyes connected with mine. "You know we have his number on file, right?"

I shook my head. "There's no way I'd use that. He'd need to give it to me himself."

A small smile tilted Frank's lips. "Is there a reason why you wouldn't ask for his number?"

I squinted at him, hating when he turned into a teacher on me. "'Everyday' Frank, please," I said.

He smiled wider. "You know I'm one and the same, right?"

I expelled a breath of air before saying, "I know, but I want an answer from my friend."

Kind, assessing eyes peered back at me. "In that case, I absolutely think you should ask for his number. You're intrigued, and he's clearly interested, and I think I know you well enough to say *nothing* should be holding you back."

I heard the emphasis loud and clear and bobbed my head.

"I need to say this though, as I can't sit on it," Frank continued, catching my attention. "Pete." He raised both brows, casting a look in the man's direction before returning his focus to me. "What's going on there?"

My eyes travelled to Pete. He sat close to Riley, saying something to make him laugh. "You caught that as well?"

"I didn't see it yesterday, but constantly today. I just can't figure it out."

There was no doubt my thoughts aligned with

Frank's. Yesterday, I'd been sure Pete had encouraged Riley to come over to me in this exact same place, but his behaviour today screamed jealous and possessive.

"Riley was confused too," I said, looking back at my friend.

"Curious." The finger tapping his lip really added to his professional persona, making me smile.

"Want to pass me my guitar while you mull that one over?" I asked, throwing him a grin.

His eyes flicked to mine, his amusement evident. "That I can do." He reached over to hand me the guitar case next to him. "I'll even vacate and go hide in the shadows to take it all in." He threw me a wink, and I wasn't quite sure if he was serious or not. Simply shaking my head at him, I watched as he walked away before pulling out my acoustic guitar and checking it remained in tune.

An hour passed by, and while Riley had not slipped into the vacant seat next to me, one of the other guys had: Carl, who also could play a mean song and sing. While disappointment had been my immediate reaction, Carl managed to pull me out of my self-pity and had me laughing at the song lyrics he'd put together.

The words tickled me as we continued to shoot

the shit and play. Finally shaking off my laughter and aware it wouldn't be long before I'd be heading for some sleep, I glanced around at the few stragglers left.

Awareness and surprise slammed into me, and if I'd been playing, I had no doubt I would have messed up the chords.

Riley sat by himself at the small picnic bench set up, which had been full the last time I'd checked. With his elbows on the table, his palms were together, bent fingers covering part of his mouth. But it was his eyes that captured my attention. They were focussed on me. What was more was he didn't look away. The intensity there sent another jolt of awareness into my veins, and I wondered just how long he'd been by himself and had his gaze on me.

Our eyes connected, and he slowly moved his hands. The nervous smile on his lips was barely there but easy to decipher.

From the little I knew about the man, it would have taken a whole heap of courage for him to stay behind. And from the focus all but flowing off him, I was the reason.

"I'm done for the night," I said to Carl, removing my gaze from Riley for the barest of moments, anxious he'd disappear in the brief break.

He was still there, which did nothing to slow down the heavy pounding of my heart.

"No worries," Carl said. "I won't be long before I turn in either. Catch you bright and early."

I nodded, casting the man a small smile before grabbing my things, guitar still in hand, and making my way over to Riley.

He sat up straighter on my approach. His hands were now palm down on the table, eyes watching my movement. The smile was still in place, but a flicker of relief appeared in his eyes.

I sat opposite him. "I didn't know you were here by yourself. If I'd known, I would have come over earlier," I admitted.

The relief shone a little brighter at my words. "I'm all good. Was enjoying watching you play." He gave a small shrug. "The others left about half an hour or so ago."

It made me all kinds of happy hearing the confirmation he'd stayed behind to hear me play. "I'd hoped to have had the chance to spend some time with you tonight," I said, making my interest loud and clear. I could never dance. Not in a nightclub, nor around my feelings. The last time I'd held back and not been honest about my feelings, it had ended in disaster. There was no way I'd do so again.

And as much as my reaction to Riley surprised me, an alien feeling of excitement made itself known. I wanted to explore that response.

The thing was, Riley seemed to be thinking the same thing, assuming I was reading him right and him staying back spoke volumes.

His smile tightened a little at my words. "I would have liked that too. Pete made it a struggle. And I didn't want to offend the guy, you know?"

I shook my head. "I don't know, honestly. What do you mean?"

A twist of his lips followed before Riley blew out a breath. His deep voice was low, the aim to keep our conversation private. "I avoid conflict like the plague. It's too easy for jabs to spiral out of control and for reactions to get out of hand, you know? If I can't walk away immediately, I'll keep my mouth shut until it's safe to do just that."

Confusion pulsed in my head. The man's words and tone were far from apathetic. Emotion laced his words, and I could only assume his response was due to him living through something that had changed him irrevocably. But did avoidance mean no conflict? At all? As in ever? Was that even possible?

How did you shut arseholes down? How did you defend those who needed support?

"Okay," I said slowly, confusion bouncing around in my brain. While I wouldn't be asking his reasons, I was curious as hell about all of my unspoken questions. Instead, I focused on the present. "So what did Pete do that got you so riled up?"

"You picked up on his behaviour earlier, I take it?"

I nodded. "Definitely. I've spent a lot of time in the group with the guy over the past eighteen months, and today was a first. He seemed jealous."

"That's what I thought too. He did say yesterday that he'd wanted a piece of you since way back when." The words seemed to pain him, his face contorted uncomfortably, his voice even lower.

"Me?" Surprise had my eyes springing wide open. "Not a chance," I said, shaking my head. "Don't get me wrong, he's eyed me up a time or two, but today was completely about you."

"What?" Riley's large shoulders tensed. And the look of horror forming on his face made me laugh, far too loudly for the situation.

"Shit, I'm sorry, but—" My laughter continued, definitely too loud for the dark campsite. I pressed my lips together as Riley squinted in my direction.

"Are you taking the piss or do you really think that?"

I grinned wide, realising he did have it in him to challenge and question when the need arose. He hadn't seemed like a pushover, so his words about conflict had confused the hell out of me.

"I really think that," I said, struggling to control the humour in my voice. "Your reaction, Riley...." I shook my head. "Priceless, mate, seriously priceless. I suppose I should be grateful," I said, leaning forwards just a fraction, sobering a little.

"Not sure I want to know, but why's that?" he asked.

"It's clear that you don't think of Pete that way, so I've got nothing to worry about." While my voice was light, I threw every ounce of honesty I could into my words.

His eyes searched mine. After a few beats of silence, he said, "Earlier you asked me a question."

I frowned, thinking over our conversations. Only one sprung to mind. "About you joining the group, coming to the regular activities and excursions?"

Riley bobbed his head. "That's the one."

I grinned, my blood racing. "So, did you make up your mind?"

"Do you attend all of the events?"

He surprised me. Again. "Most of them, for sure. I help Frank organise everything, so we make sure it doesn't conflict with what either of us has going on."

"In that case, yes. I'm interested."

My heart pounded loudly, making it difficult to form a response. Between my fuzzy brain and my twitching cock, all I could do was smile and nod. Somehow I managed a quiet "Sounds good." Then I remembered my phone.

Tugging it out of my pocket and almost dropping it in my haste, I threw Riley a sheepish smile. Pleased to see him grinning at me, I relaxed a little, able to catch my breath. "Can I have your number?"

"To talk to me about the next event?" he asked.

I shook my head. "No, we do that via email. Your number's for me."

He smirked, the first legit smirk I'd seen on him in the past two days. This one screamed of quiet confidence, and I was eager to see more of this side of him.

Bobbing his head, he said, "I'd like that. Just make sure you text me so I have yours too."

I whipped together a text, not wanting to wait, already looking forwards to getting to know Riley without the group as our spectators.

THREE DAYS SINCE I'D SOMEHOW MANAGED TO MAKE IT to the top of the climbing rock, and the ache every time I crouched had finally eased. The whole weekend motivated me to get a little fitter. I wasn't interested in standing on scales, but exercising regularly so I wouldn't be rolling in pain after the next Outback Boys meetup sounded like a good plan, as did not losing my ability to speak from breathlessness.

Life returned to normal, a given since going away for a weekend wasn't so unusual for most people, but it was new and invigorating for me. So despite me still rolling out of bed as usual, getting on with my tasks for the day, having lunch with Pete, where he was acting like nothing about his behaviour had been odd a few days earlier, then returning home—all absolutely the norm—the differences were evident.

Not only was I walking on the beach after work, but I was cooking my food rather than relying on takeout or pre-prepared meals. Or at least I was giving it a good effort.

Then there was the text I'd just received.

The sight of Aiden's name pulled me up short as I stepped out of my car for my new daily walk. My heart fluttered, reminding me I'd been hoping for his text and had been too chickenshit to reach out to him.

Aiden: Recovered from the weekend yet?

Rather than overthink it, which I was more than prone to do, I tapped out a message.

Me: Only just. It took a while.

I kicked off my thongs as soon as my feet hit the sand, then looked at my phone at the new message.

Aiden: "Just" sounds good to me. What you been up to?

Me: Work. Just got to the beach for a walk.

Aiden: Nice. Which one?

Me: Noosa.

Aiden: Wow, and you were able to find somewhere to park? Impressive.

I laughed. A beautiful beach with golden sand, it was popular and crazy busy during the tourist season especially. Once, I'd spent an hour looking for a parking spot, but the beach was one of my favourites. And at this time of day, things were relatively quiet.

Me: Shocker, right? How about you? Busy?

Aiden: Fairly steady. Same old routine.

I hesitated, wondering how to respond, what to say next. I didn't want to cut the contact short, but I wasn't a fan of texting or phone calls. Nor did I really want empty conversation. I huffed out a breath, knowing I was doing it again.

Overthinking was a curse.

Aiden: I have some free time on Saturday afternoon. Do you want to meet up for coffee?

An immediate smile pulled my lips high. I paused at the lapping waves, burying my feet in the sand as the water surrounded my ankles.

Me: Yeah. Sounds good. You want to meet somewhere halfway?

While I didn't know exactly where he lived, I knew there was over an hour's drive separating us.

Aiden: That would be great. Do you want me to pick somewhere and let you know?

Me: Sounds good.

Aiden: Will do. I've got to go, but I'll let you know tomorrow.

Aiden: Stay out of trouble until then. No tripping over loose rocks or anything. :)

I snorted, recalling how I'd done just that on Monday before I'd climbed the rock face. I'd sworn blind the rock had jumped out at me. Apparently, Aiden hadn't believed me and had offered to look at my feet. I'd suggested he was using it as an excuse to check out my size. My words had fallen right on out there, leaving me pink-cheeked and Aiden laughing.

He'd promised he was looking for two left feet, but I didn't miss the interest in his eyes or the increased flirtation between the two of us.

Me: I'll see what I can do. Have a good night.

Aiden: You too.

Pocketing my phone, I carried on with my walk, enjoying the warm water and the fresh spray.

At thirty-six, guys had come and gone, but nothing had truly stuck. The past couple of years, I hadn't put myself out there at all.

Fitting in had never come easily to me, and while I was aware of the strong LGBTQIA+ community in my area, it was easier for me to stand on the sidelines and watch from afar.

Joining this outdoor activity group was my first

attempt to push my boundaries and truly step out of my comfort zone. And I had Pete to thank for that.

And then there was Aiden. We'd got on surprisingly well. The possibility of us becoming friends had me grinning, inhaling deeply, and enjoying my walk even more.

I seriously lacked in the friends department. There was Pete, but as co-workers, we were friendly and other than this past weekend, we didn't really see each other out of work hours. Not for his lack of trying, though.

I finished my walk not long after and headed to the store to buy some fresh veggies before heading home. The whole time, I thought about seeing Aiden again, relishing in the buzz of excitement licking across my skin. This weekend couldn't come soon enough.

I SHUT MY MAC AND STRETCHED, RELIEVED IT WAS Friday afternoon and time to head home. The week had been busier than I'd anticipated, with a development in one of the programs needing to be rolled out. The research institute where I worked was a good place to be, especially as the organisation was doing so much good in medical research.

After this full-on week, my brain buzzed from dealing with the complicated bioinformatic pipelines that needed some TLC.

"You heading straight home?" Pete asked as he packed up his desk, ready for the weekend.

"After a walk on the beach, yeah. My head's too wired to go straight home."

He bobbed his head in my direction. "Right, that add-on was a nightmare."

"That it was." I grabbed my keys and my lunch cooler and pushed my chair under my workspace. "Right, have a good weekend." I lifted my hand into a small wave but stopped when he started speaking.

"I'm coming now. I'll walk down with you."

I hovered near the door as he grabbed his things and made his way over. When he reached my side, he headed towards the lift. "Actually," I said, "I was going to take the stairs."

Pete cast me a quick glance before shrugging. "No worries."

We veered in the direction of the staircase and started making our way down the five flights of stairs. Every day this week I'd used the stairs to get to and from the office. I still panted on the way up, but it was getting easier.

"Any plans this weekend?"

For the first time ever, I hesitated with my answer. Usually, it was a general "Not a lot," but since I was meeting up with Aiden, I expected I'd get a reaction of some sort. I just didn't know what kind.

"Not a lot," I settled on. "Probably get some more walking in, grab a coffee or something." Since I wasn't technically lying, I didn't feel too uneasy about keeping the specifics of my plans to myself.

Truth was, I was set to meet Aiden at a Gympie coffee shop at two in the afternoon. Just the thought of it sent a whisper of excitement fluttering in my stomach. The sensation both bolstered me while making me ridiculously nervous.

"Sounds relaxing."

I side-eyed him. His gaze was straight ahead, and he didn't seem to have caught on to the ripple of tension in my responses.

"That's the plan," I answered, pleased to be reaching the main foyer. I tugged out my ID and swiped it over the scanner before I headed out the exit, Pete close behind and doing the same thing. "What about you?" I asked, remembering to be polite, despite wanting to get away and to the beach as quickly as possible. I couldn't help feeling antsy around him since last weekend. While he'd been absolutely his usual self all week, his odd behaviour was hard to ignore or forget.

"I promised to visit my sister and niece."

I smiled at that, thinking of the photos he'd shown me of Georgie, his three-year-old niece. It was clear the guy doted on her.

"Yeah? That should be fun."

When his response was a shrug, I paused a few steps away from my car, turning to him. "What's wrong?" For the first time really all week, I took a good look at Pete. Dark circles sat under his eyes. He looked seriously tired. Not only that, while he'd cracked the same sort of jokes around the office all week, when I thought about it, there'd been something slightly off about his tone. The knowledge that something wasn't quite right punched me in the gut. I'd been a shit friend.

"Nothing," he said a little too quickly and without a shred of believability.

My brows shot high at the bullshit answer. There were times to push and times to keep my mouth shut, and from his inability to make eye contact for more than a brief glance, I knew it was the latter. So while I didn't call him out, I offered, "Okay, but if there's anything you need, you know you can call me, yeah?"

He bobbed his head and swallowed hard, the action telling and worrying. "Yeah, thanks. Appreciate it. Best be off. Have a good weekend." Turning, he strolled away with no sass, no jokes, and not at all acting like Pete.

I released a heavy sigh as I got into my car, starting the engine and turning the air-con to full. Unease swirled in my gut, right alongside guilt for not being honest with Pete while also being ignorant to whatever shit was going on for him to be behaving uncharacteristically.

I drove out of my space, seeing Pete standing at his car, staring at his phone in his hand, a deep crease between his brows.

Fuck, there was no way I could drive away with him like this. Quickly pulling alongside the boot of his car, effectively blocking him in, I lowered my window. Pete glanced in my direction, his eyes widening when he spotted me.

"You okay?" he asked, pocketing his phone.

"Yeah, all good. But get your arse in the car and come for a walk with me." He opened his mouth to speak, but I stopped him, reasonably sure he was going to turn me down. "Seriously, butt in the car now. I'll even buy you a drink." His lips curled at that. I rarely went into bars.

With a bob of his head, he threw his stuff in his car, locked it, and made his way around to the passenger side. Once he was strapped in, I pulled away, heading to Noosa.

We kept quiet the whole way, me never needing to make idle conversation and Pete unexpectedly not yammering away. And that was fine. There was no hardship in comfortable silences, and I expected every now and then it was good for Pete too.

We found a parking spot in the national park, then headed first to pick up a takeout coffee before heading to the beach. There was a strong easterly wind, bringing with it the scent of seawater. It was warm against my skin, and I was relieved I wore a short-sleeved shirt with my dress shorts. Thankfully the sand had cooled enough so it wasn't hot on my feet, but still, we edged close to the water, allowing the gentle waves to lap over our feet and up to our ankles.

The silence remained, the sound of the waves and the whistle in the wind enough to keep us company. I looked out to sea, spotting a couple of boats in the distance and a couple of surfboards, no doubt holidaymakers since there was little in the way of waves.

"Mina has breast cancer."

Pete's quiet voice startled me, and it took a moment for his words to hit home.

"She was diagnosed two weeks ago." He shook his head and continued to walk. I closed my eyes at the news, waiting to see if he'd finished speaking or not. After a beat, he continued. "It's invasive, stage four. She's having a double mastectomy on Monday."

"Holy shit, Pete," I said, unable to stay quiet any longer. "I'm so sorry, mate. Shit."

He bobbed his head. "At some point after that, they'll be starting her on chemo, but the prognosis isn't good." I glanced over at him, and he looked away. Immediately, I reached out to him, putting my arm around him. He stopped on contact, and I wrapped him up, my arms folding around him with ease with his slight frame and shorter height.

His grip was fierce, holding on with a strength that surprised me.

The poor guy was hurting.

I hugged him wordlessly, not offering any placating words that were really about me and not him. And a sister.... I swallowed back my emotion, knowing all too well the agony of loss. That shit ripped you raw to the point of threatening to keep you bleeding. And it took one hell of an amount of strength to move to the point of living again.

When he relaxed his arms, I eased away, knowing he was ready for a breath. He didn't look at me as he started walking, nor did he say a word. He didn't have to.

"I told Maxine today I'd be needing some compassionate leave to look after Georgie."

"Any problems with that?" I asked, hoping like hell there wasn't. Mina was a single mum. While I knew they didn't have family around, I wasn't sure the whys of it or even if they were still alive. We were workmates, not close buddies, and beyond general shooting the shit, we knew little about each other.

"It was all good. It's only a couple of days' compassionate leave I can be granted, but I've got sick days saved up, so will take those as well. Maxine's cool and didn't push, letting me know she'd do whatever she could to support me."

I huffed out a breath, my emotions high and draining. "That's good. You going to move into her place?"

"Yeah, for a while," he said. "We'll just keep playing it by ear and take each day as it comes, you know?" His voice was unsteady as he spoke, but he was making an impressive effort at keeping his shit together. "Georgie's in day care, so I'll keep her in there so I can be with Mina." He tilted his head back and shook his head. "Shit, you mind if we throw the coffee and I get that beer now?"

A sad smile formed on my lips. "Course not. Let's go."

We turned in the direction of town, heading towards one of the bars, and for the first time in a while, I consider screwing off my sobriety and consoling Pete by having a drink with him. As soon as the idea formed, ice filled my veins and nausea brewed in my gut.

There was no chance of that happening. Not in this lifetime.

By the time I got home, exhaustion had swept over me with the force of a tidal wave. Emotionally spent, I got myself a glass of water and headed out to my small back veranda to watch the night draw fully in. Once settled, I took a large gulp of water and pulled out my phone, aware I'd received a message on my way home.

When I saw Aiden's name, a thrill of excitement zapped me like lightning, momentarily reducing my tiredness and the sorrow that had taken up residence.

Aiden: I hope you managed to get a walk in today and survived your Friday. See you tomorrow at 2.

My mouth curled up into a small smile. While nerves still fluttered a little uncontrollably at the idea of seeing him again, eager anticipation was at the forefront. I already had a plan in my head to take it slow and not rush into anything, self-preservation being the driving force.

Me connecting with someone, especially so quickly, was rare, but I'd been hurt too many times in the past to be able to bounce back should I fall and not be caught.

That didn't mean I wasn't looking forwards to seeing him again and getting to know the guy. With that in mind, I texted him back.

Me: I did, thanks. Not long got back. I hope you had a good day. Looking forwards to tomorrow.

I hit Send immediately, not wanting to overthink my words and end up deleting and retyping. Almost immediately, three dancing dots appeared. That you could tell when someone had their cursor in the message box was one pretty cool tech development. But with it came its own drawbacks, like that awful time when you saw the dots bouncing to only stop, to restart and do the same multiple times, only to never receive the text.

Yeah, that part sucked arse for sure.

His message appeared, and I grinned at the simple fact of receiving it.

Aiden: A late one, huh. I hope it wasn't because you spent an hour looking for parking. ;P

I chuckled.

Me: Nope. Ended up having a friend come with me, grabbed a drink after. Went wild and had a Sprite.

As soon as I hit Send, my gut flipped a little, not only because of Pete and his shit news but because I hadn't mentioned who I was with. I'd deliberately been evasive. I now had a better understanding of Pete's strange behaviour last weekend. That wasn't the case for Aiden. As far as he was concerned, Pete was acting jealous.

That was so far from the truth that it wasn't even funny. In many ways, I wished that's what the problem was.

It took five long minutes before Aiden

responded, but no dancing dots drove me crazy, which was something.

Aiden: Pleased you had company. See you tomorrow.

I expelled a breath, not quite liking the feeling of not fully disclosing, but between being drained from Pete's sharing, which despite the heavy load I was pleased he had, I just didn't have anything more in me tonight.

Plus, the bottom line was Pete had needed someone and that I could offer him the venting space he needed was the right thing to do.

Feeling too tired to cook the veggie lasagne I had planned, I threw a potato in the air fryer and switched on the barbie to cook my steak. After eating, I planned to zone out in front of Stan or Netflix before I passed out.

I didn't want to be spending too much time with my thoughts; not tonight. That would just get me thinking about Tanya, which was more than I could handle on a Friday night by myself.

By the time morning came and went, nervous excitement churned in my stomach. I was already in Gympie and was thirty minutes early. Hanging around at home had driven me nuts. It made sense to take the short trip here instead and fill my time wandering around the town before meeting up with Aiden.

I stopped into a small homeware store in Mary Street, not interested in buying anything but looking for a distraction. Once finished and probably looking at the same photo frame for far too long, I left with a smile and thanks before moving on. One foot over the threshold of a small clothing store, I paused when I heard my name. A quick glance told me it was Aiden.

His smile was bright when he looked at me. Immediately, I turned and made my way over, saying, "Hey, how're things?"

He bobbed his head, making eye contact, the connection there enough to make me swallow before his gaze roamed the rest of my face, seemingly to get his fill.

Heat bloomed in my chest, and I couldn't help but follow suit.

Last week, covered in sweat, mud, and another time soaked in river water, Aiden was all levels of attractive. The man before me, though, had clearly made an effort.

Freshly shaven, his lips appeared more plump, distinguished, hell, pink even. I had no idea the right word to describe them. But my gaze snagged on them, and I wondered what it would be like to kiss him. What his lips would feel like. Firm or soft; maybe a perfect combination of the two?

"Hey, Riley, you look good," Aiden said in greeting.

My gaze flicked to his at his compliment, the rush of heat travelling at warp speed when I saw only honesty in his eyes. "Thanks," I answered, a little self-consciously. "You look pretty good your-self," I offered, willing the warmth in my cheeks to dissipate. And he really did. He was dressed in a plain tee that fitted nicely, just clinging in the slightest way to reveal his defined arms. His dark jeans were smart, looking well kept and close to new.

I wore something similar, and when I moved my attention to his feet, I smiled when I spotted he wore thongs, just like I did, the weather heating up just on this side of uncomfortable for closed-in shoes.

"I know I'm early, but do you want to grab a coffee now, or do you have things to do?"

Rather than make up an excuse about why I was also here early, I nodded. "We can go now for sure. I was just browsing."

Aiden indicated with an outstretched arm for us to head towards the coffee shop. As we walked, he picked up the conversation. "I was early too.

Thought it better I make a good impression rather than be late."

I side-eyed him with a small twitch of my lips. "I appreciate that. Being late drives me up the wall," I admitted. "I'd rather be an hour early than ten minutes late."

His laughter was deep and happy sounding, flowing over me and giving me goosebumps. It was a good sound. "I hear you. My pops is a stickler for timekeeping. Would tan my hide if I was ever late home as a kid." He shrugged, seeming happy with the memory.

"Obviously left its mark," I said good-naturedly.

"Ha. It did that. And it's paying off, since I get to spend an extra twenty minutes with you ahead of time."

I couldn't contain my smile at his sweetness. The hint of flirt in his words was cute, but nothing too full-on or uncomfortable. I was curious about his grandad, though, wondering if he'd been the one to bring Aiden up. Not that I'd be asking, as I had no desire to talk about my own parents back in Perth. What I did ask was "Your grandad's glad to have moved, settled in well enough? I know you said it's been over a year or something, but from what you told me about working on the station, it must be different."

"Yeah, he's good," Aiden answered as we arrived at the open-front coffee shop. Before he could respond more, we reached the counter.

Once in front of the shiny metal counter complete with a cabinet flowing with sweet treats, I asked, "I'll get these. What'll it be?"

Aiden flicked a glance at me, his smile a little shyer than previous. "Will you judge me if I ask for almond milk and honey iced coffee?"

Wide-eyed, I did a piss-poor job at hiding my surprise at his drink order. "Uhm, no," I answered. "No judgement here."

He chuckled. "Not what you were expecting?"

I gave a shrug and scrunched my nose, admitting, "Perhaps I should be asking you not to judge me for assuming you'd go for a simple black coffee or maybe a flat white?"

His chuckle turned into a snort. "Not sure if I should be insulted or flattered by that." There was zero offense in his tone with his wide grin and the humour alight in his eyes.

"Let's just go with flattered, and I'll get you your drink. You want a cake or—" I scanned the glass-fronted display fridge. "—a pastry or something?"

With a shake of his head, Aiden said, "No. I'm good, thanks. I'll grab a seat near the fan. Sound okay?"

"Great." I watched him go, unable to pull my gaze away from him. Those jeans did seriously look good on him.

I turned to the server when she greeted me and ordered our drinks before making my way to Aiden. He'd chosen a cosy booth with cushioned seats and a curved bench so we could sit as close or as far away from each other as we wished.

I rolled my eyes at myself, needing to simply sit down without overthinking exactly where I should sit. Scooting into the booth, I opted for opposite. This way, we could have a conversation without angling.

"So, your grandad," I prompted. "You said he was good?"

Aiden smiled, leaning back against the booth's cushion, looking very much comfortable in his own skin. "He is. Despite the old goat's grumbles, not being so isolated, nor as hot and dry, is good for him. As long as he can see gold and red soil and hear cows bellowing, he's at home."

"There are worse animals to keep you company, for sure."

He chuckled at that. "There sure are. He's getting on now. Gonna be celebrating his eighty-seventh birthday in a few months."

"Oh, wow." I wondered how Aiden managed that, whether his grandad needed extra care or something. While we'd spent a fair amount of time talking when kayaking, there were years of stories left untouched. "And he still gets around okay?"

Aiden bobbed his head. "The man's too stubborn not to. I've had to ban him from the quad bikes, have actually had to hide the keys."

My eyes widened at that. "Seriously?"

"Yeah. He doesn't know how to stop or take no for an answer at times, but he fell off a quad before we moved out east. Miraculously came out unscathed. No idea how the man didn't break a hip or something. Stubbornness, I expect." Aiden was shaking his head, but his whole face was lit with fondness.

"He sounds like quite the character."

"He is that. My nephew calls him Boo-Boo," he said with a snort, while I filed away that he had more family. "Whenever he visited, Pops always had some sort of injury. It was one of Timmy's first words." He chuckled and then looked up at the server approaching with our drinks. We both said thanks, and I eyed his coffee concoction.

"You wanna try some, huh?"

I grinned. "I'm curious."

He nudged his drink over. "Go for it."

"You sure?" I couldn't remember the last time I'd tried anyone's drink or food or shared anything. It felt almost intimate. I held on to the straw and started to pull it up.

"I don't mind sharing."

His words had me shooting a surprised glance his way. "O-kay." I wasn't sure where else to go with it.

"I promise I don't have cooties or anything. Regular checks here."

I choked on my spit, since I hadn't had a chance to take a suck yet. I hacked, face heating, eyes going teary, and my heart threatening to burst out of my chest.

"Shit, mate. Sorry," Aiden said, reaching out to me as though to pound my back. I stopped him quickly with a shake of my head and a half-arsed smile, my throat raw, but at least I was getting my breath back as I calmed and drew in air. "Seriously, I'm sorry. I can't believe I said that." He stood abruptly, and I caught my breath, not sure what was happening. My shoulders relaxed when I realised he'd stopped at the water station and was filling up a glass. A few moments later, he returned with a glass of water, placing it in front of me.

When he sat, his eyes seemed dimmer somehow, worry creased his brow, and red sat high on his cheeks.

"Thanks," I croaked, indicating the water and taking a few sips. After another deep breath, I took a big gulp and exhaled. I chuckled and wiped at my eyes. "Nothing like choking on air, right?" I deliberately focussed on him, ensuring eye contact, wanting to reassure Aiden I was fine. Hell, I was the one who was crazy embarrassed.

Aiden's smile was tight. He closed his eyes in a long blink before returning his gaze to me. "I'm really sorry. That was so inappropriate, and well... yeah." He lifted his hand and rubbed it over his head. It landed on the back of his scalp, where he held it and rubbed there a beat before he scrubbed his hand over his mouth. The poor guy was seriously mortified.

"Honestly, it's fine. Just kinda took me by surprise, is all."

He winced.

"Seriously, Aiden." I reached out, my need to

ease the concern in his eyes pushing me to take action. My hand landed on his forearm. His skin was warm, surprisingly soft, and I could feel his sinewy muscles. Aiden's eyes dropped to my hand. My fingers twitched in reaction, contemplating moving, but I stayed true, my desire to see him let this go too strong. "It's oversharing we can laugh about together, yeah. You can tell the story of your faux pas, and I can tell mine of you making me forget how to breathe."

When his gaze connected with mine, his eyes were filled with an intensity that surprised me. But I didn't sever contact. "Okay," he said with a heavy breath. "Thanks." A small smile curved his lips. While it didn't quite reach his eyes, it did shed some of the tension previously there.

"So," I said, finally breaking contact as I reached out for his iced drink, "now I know that you're cootie free, which honestly, what even are cooties, seriously?" His smile stretched wider. "So yeah, I promise I'm cootie free." I placed the straw in my mouth and sucked. So caught up in not choking, then smoothing over Aiden's embarrassment, I'd all but forgotten the whole point of me sharing the same straw as him—that was, until the honey-flavoured coffee hit my tongue. The combination of the sweet with the bitter, along with the distinct taste of almond, was delicious. My eyes widened in surprise. Releasing the straw, I swallowed, saying, "Damn, that's good."

Aiden's cheeks lifted high, and the tension from moments ago seemed to disappear. "Right? So no judgement about my drink choice then?"

I shook my head. "No judgement here as long as I get one of these next time."

A spark lit in his eyes. "As long as it's my treat, then we can definitely make that happen."

My heart did a little flip, more than happy with that, liking we'd already decided that there'd be a next time. "So how'd you discover this drink?" I asked.

"Actually, my sister's ex introduced me. She couldn't drink or eat dairy. Kinda got me hooked."

"There are worse things an ex could leave behind, right?"

Aiden snorted at that. "For sure. Trina, Emily's ex, was all right. She had good taste in coffee. My sister made the right call, though. She wouldn't have Timmy now either."

"How old's your nephew?"

"He's six in a couple of months. He rules the

roost and keeps his parents on their toes; hell, all of us on our toes."

"With you as his uncle, I can only imagine." I laughed, quirking my right brow high at him.

"Hey, now. I'm the sane and steady one. Everyone else is trouble incarnate."

"Why don't I quite believe that?" I asked, a noticeable edge of flirtation weaving its way into my words as we continued.

"Okay, now, *now*, in my wizened years, I'm the sane and steady one. Hell, Campbell, my brother-in-law, competes in rodeo professionally." Both of my brows shot up high at that. He continued, "You see, you're now seeing how I'm the one who's not insane, right?"

"For sure. Rodeo is intense."

"You been to one?"

"Yeah, when I was in Perth."

"Boddington, right?"

I laughed. "That's the one." Considering his brother-in-law's profession, I wasn't surprised he'd heard about the rodeo in Boddington. It drew in the crowds as a yearly event, and I was sure it was the biggest rodeo event in Western Australia.

"My sister and her family travel all around for

events, both here and overseas, mainly the States. They have a permanent home in Maryborough, though. It's one of the reasons why I headed this way, dragging my pops kicking and screaming. Or at least pretending to. He would never admit it, but he was excited about seeing his great-grandson more often."

"That's nice. It's good that you're closer."

"It was a good move, for sure."

We finished up our drinks, continuing to talk about his family and his property. We ventured into chatting about my job and spoke about the next meetup for the Outback Boys. It was taking place in two weekends' time, but this time just a day trip. And when he pulled out his phone and went into the group's Dropbox folder, passing it to me to make sure I signed up for the day's hike, I expected I'd start to become a regular simply so I could spend more time with Aiden.

There was something disarming about him. The quiet confidence. The sweet, flirty banter that he eased into conversations smoothly, despite his foot-in-mouth moment earlier. Though truthfully, the fact he'd told me that had filled me with both warmth and need. Nothing said "I'm interested" more than stating a clean bill of health. It did wonders for my ego, something that didn't show its face very often.

"So, what are your plans for the rest of the day?" he asked as we finished up our second drink. I'd gone for a soft drink this time.

I shrugged. "Not a lot. May go for a walk on the beach, stretch my legs a bit, you know? How about you?"

With something I could only describe as interest in his eyes, his gaze roamed mine. "Nothing planned. My pops is at my sister's for the day, and I think is staying overnight."

When he finished speaking, the air charged, felt heavy with the silence and his words. Did he want to spend time with me? Was he not ready to cut our time together short? The possibility had heat dancing across my skin. Not quite the rush of warmth from other times, though. This heat was gentle in its spread, a flickering of a flame not quite ready to combust, simply reaching out and trying to grasp for the oxygen needed to expand.

When I didn't respond immediately, there was a subtle shift in his shoulders, perhaps the slightest of sags. If my attention hadn't been so fixed on him, I would have missed it.

Shit. Disappointment and a quiet acceptance

seemed to reach his eyes. That's not what I wanted. Far from it.

"You can come," I spluttered—almost damn shouted—in my haste to get my words out and remove that look from his eyes. "I mean, if you want to do something... with me. We could go to the beach together, or not, something else if you want." I pressed my lips together, my breathing picking up speed a little.

And there it was, the change I'd been hoping for. Aiden's whole face transformed with my blurted offer. The smile lifted the balls of his cheeks high. His eyes came alight, all but sparkling in the way he looked at me.

"Yeah," he answered, his words soft despite the gruffness present. "I'd really like that."

I grinned, not willing to hold back the charge of excitement his response gave me. "Great, you want to get out of here now?"

He bobbed his head, picking up his drink and finishing it off. "That sounds good."

I shuffled out of the booth, Aiden following suit. Side by side, we headed out of the coffee house together, the brush of his shoulder against mine nothing short of electrifying, comforting in the spark and connection.

Jesus, I liked him. A lot. My thoughts from earlier seemed to mock me, about not rushing into anything, but it wasn't like we were standing here making out. Though the idea of doing just that had merit, for sure.

I cleared my throat, getting my thoughts back on track. "Anywhere in particular you want to go?" I asked, aware he'd had the longer journey out of the two of us; plus if we headed south towards my neck of the woods, he'd have even further to travel.

"Honestly, I'm easy. As long as I get the time to spend with you, I'm golden."

Pleasure bubbled in my gut at his words as I searched my memory for the best place to go. While I'd lived on the Sunny Coast for a few years, Gympie and beyond was a little farther north than I was used to travelling.

"How about Rainbow Beach?" It would probably take an hour. I winced at that and looked at the time. It was just after four. "Shit, I didn't realise it was so late." He glanced over to see the time on my phone.

He grunted. "Two hours sure does fly by, right?" His disappointment mirrored my own. Heading to Rainbow Beach now would be crazy. It was too late in the day.

We paused, shifting to the side so as not to block

the pavement. "Okay...." I trailed off, my brain working overtime. The beach was out, but it didn't mean we couldn't do something else. "Bowling?" I asked hesitantly. No idea where that idea had come from. I couldn't remember the last time I'd been ten pin bowling, but I was sure there'd be one locally.

He nodded immediately. "Yeah, sounds good."

With that, we headed to our cars while I searched for the location on my phone, and when we went our separate ways, having parked in different places, I made the quick call to secure us a couple of games and drove off with butterflies in my stomach and a lightness in my chest.

Chapter Six

AIDEN

My laugh was loud as it rang out in the bowling place. It turned out I was useless at bowling. And I didn't mind one bit, as it seemed my disastrous throws were a source of amusement for the both of us. Not only that, but my stomach ached from laughing so hard, my cheeks hurt, and I couldn't remember feeling so at ease or entertained in a long time.

But it was more than that. Every time Riley snorted a laugh or gave me a half-arsed consolatory pat on the back, that lightness in my chest grew and felt pretty spectacular.

Riley was amazing and so unexpected. At some time between eating french fries, throwing another gutter ball, and laughing with Riley about shit we got up to as kids, I'd decided I was more than okay with unexpected.

When I'd messaged Riley asking him to meet up with coffee, I'd been excited to see him again and at the idea of getting to know him better. He was easy on the eyes and had the type of body that could wrap me up and hold me with ease if we ever got to that point—something I'd never had with anyone before, specifically James. But rather than any thought or comparison of James punching me in the gut, for the first time I admitted to myself that Riley was different, and I was different with him, and I was good with that.

"Perhaps I should ask if they have a special scoreboard for lowest points achieved," I joked, eyeing my number nineteen.

Riley smirked, looking at the board and my number. "Well, there's still two more bowls left."

I shook my head and threw him a grin. "It would take a bloody miracle for me to show an improvement now." I wasn't kidding. This was our second game. The first I'd received such low scores that the old lady two lanes over gave me a kind smile and offered to buy me a beer, figuring I could do with a pick-me-up. Riley had chuckled the whole time, while I'd thanked her for her kind offer but turned her down.

At the moment, on the eighth bowl of our second game, there was only one other lane in session. It was that weird sort of time, I expected, with it being dinner time.

"I've offered to help twice," Riley shot back at me, a good-natured smile on his face. He wasn't condescending in his offer, but I knew he found the whole thing hilarious.

With my right brow arched high, I turned and faced him. "So, when you say you'll help, is that a smooth move to snuggle up behind me and show me how to bend my knees and release?" My lips twitched by the time I finished speaking, barely holding back my amusement, as he blushed right alongside his snort of laughter.

"Guess I'm not as smooth as I thought, huh," Riley said with a head shake. His hand reached for his pocket, and he winced.

"You okay?"

"Yeah, sorry."

"For?"

"My phone keeps vibrating." He rolled his eyes at my wide eyes. "And no, that's not a euphemism."

I chuckled. "Someone keeps calling you? Go ahead and check if you need to."

Riley hesitated. "You sure you don't mind?"

I liked that he'd asked. I liked even more that it had been ringing for a while but he'd left it alone rather than pulling it out and dealing with it. While I relied on my phone for many things, little pissed me off more than being ignored by a person because they had their head buried in their phone.

My thoughts immediately flashed to James, remembering the pointless arguments we'd had, usually when eating dinner or doing something together, and he'd done exactly that—focused on the phone rather than taking the time to simply be present.

That Riley made an effort to be present—first day and good impressions or not—mattered. A lot.

While he checked his phone, I picked up my Sprite and took a swig of the sugary drink. It was when I heard a whispered, "Shit," that I turned my attention back to Riley.

A frown marred his usually smooth brow. He then huffed out a breath, his gaze angling towards me.

"What's wrong?"

As he stood, he winced. "I'm so sorry. That was Pete."

Surprise rippled along my skin. From what I'd learned about his friendship with Pete last weekend and our hours of conversation, they were work friends more than anything, and they rarely saw each other or spoke out of work. "Everything okay?" I asked, already assuming the answer was no based on his facial expression.

He shook his head. "Not really. He's left a message saying his sister is in the hospital. I think he's freaking out."

"That doesn't sound good." I hesitated before saying, "Do you need to go?"

A heavy exhale preceded his words. "Yeah, I think I do. He has a lot on at the moment and is struggling."

I bobbed my head, showing my understanding though not really feeling it. Confusion swarmed my thoughts. "Yeah, sure. Of course. If he needs support, you need to be there to help him, for sure." There was nothing else I could say, no questions to ask without sounding like a prick.

"I'm so sorry to be cutting this short." Genuine remorse seemed to fill his features, and my own tendril of guilt pushed to the surface that I was being such a sook.

"I think it's safe to say you were kicking my arse." I offered a smile, trying to lighten the tension rolling off him.

He chuckled. It was quiet, but I was happy I'd pulled it from him. "True, but…" He paused, falling silent a beat before picking back up with "I wasn't ready to finish our time quite yet." A shrug followed, sweet and small from this gentle giant of a man.

His words hit their mark, sending a flush of contentment down to the tips of my toes. "Me either," I admitted, "but we'll do it again." I left my statement hang there but not for long before he smiled.

"I'd like that. Just let me know when you're free, and I'll make it happen."

We cleared up the area and removed the godawful bowling shoes, replacing them at the counter. Once at the cars, parked side by side, I turned to him, the crackle of tension between us heady. My gut tightened in anticipation.

"So," I said a little gruffly and not as smoothly as I'd hoped. Alongside the tension, I was nervous as hell, frustrating me to no end. I swallowed before saying, "I hope Pete's sister is okay."

"Thanks."

"I'm usually shit on the phone," I continued, drawing a smile from Riley, "but if you call, I'll answer."

His gaze softened, and he took a step forwards. My breath caught at the movement, my anticipation mounting, turning into something tangible—a need to have my mouth on his.

We met in the middle—both taking a shuffling step and leaning forwards. Our lips touched once, then twice; I parted my mouth slightly on the third connection, Riley matching my movements with an ease not lost on me.

I moved my hand to his waist, my fingers around his back, and I put the slightest pressure there. His mouth slid over mine, this time deeper, sending a flurry of wings to take flight in my stomach. Warm, soft, and the perfect pressure, I fell into the kiss, not holding back my rumble of approval when one of his hands moved to the back of my head, the other to my waist.

A wave of desire flashed to life at the sensation of Riley's large hands feeling so damn right on my body. We pulled apart almost simultaneously at the sound of a vehicle entering the car park. Neither of us looked away, though, our gazes connecting.

Immediately, I smiled, and he soon mirrored the action. Pink dotted the top of his cheeks, and I reached out and brushed my thumb over his right cheekbone, enjoying the quick bob of his Adam's apple at the contact.

"Call me later or tomorrow?" I asked, not holding back how much I wanted him to do just that.

"Definitely. Tomorrow, if I'm not home till late." His gaze roamed mine, then traced my face, landing on my mouth. My lips quirked a moment before he pressed his over them once more before stepping back. He huffed out a breath, telling me everything I needed to know.

He felt this too.

"Drive safe," I said, forcing my legs to move away from him rather than towards him.

After a beat, he headed to the driver side of his car. "You too."

With one last lingering look, intensity clear as day in his eyes, he ducked his head and got in his car. I held up my hand in a wave, opening my ute door as I watched him go, already eager for his call and the next time I could have his mouth on mine.

"W HAT THE HELL HAS CRAWLED UP YOUR ARSE?"

I jolted at my pops's question, whacking my elbow in the process and cursing.

Apparently that was funny, as Pops stood there snorting at me and shaking his head. "Perhaps it's time to give up, boy. Get your butt inside and grab a cold drink before you do more damage than good." He turned without waiting for my response, a slight limp in his left leg as he did so.

I huffed out a breath, knowing the old man was right. I'd been working on replacing the fan belt on my tractor for a couple of hours, which was a lot longer than it should have taken me. My concentration was for shit.

After enjoying every moment of my afternoon with Riley and ending it the way that we did, I'd returned home with a buzz of adrenalin that I hadn't felt in a long time. It had stayed with me through the night and until this morning. Two in the afternoon had come and gone, and he still hadn't called. My mood had plummeted to the point I was like a bear with a bad head. Truth was, I was grumpy as fuck and had spent the past three hours annoyed with myself that I simply didn't pick up the phone and give Riley a call while mentally clipping myself on the upside of my head that I was being a turd for all but pining over him not calling yet.

It had been one date. One fun afternoon. And while I'd thought the kiss had been epic, Riley didn't owe me anything. I also hadn't a clue what time he'd got in or what had happened with Pete and his sister, so me being a whiney arse additionally pissed me off.

And with all of that, I couldn't help but be curious about Pete. For a while, I'd known the guy, had actually met him my first time at Outback Boys when I joined this chapter. He seemed like a decent bloke, a bit full-on at times, and while I didn't really feel the pull to get to know him better, nothing about him offended me. Except for last weekend's weirdness about Riley.

And that was the crux. While Riley didn't believe it, I had an inkling Pete had a hard-on for him.

After I finished packing my tools away, I headed inside. Pops had already pulled me a tinny out, a Blue Marlin, a non-alcoholic beer he knew I liked.

"Your sister said she was coming over next Friday and dropping Timmy off for the night. I said we'd have him till Saturday afternoon."

I bobbed my head, already realizing that any chance of meeting up with Riley was out of the question in that case. A thread of disappointment slithered down my spine. But me seeing him again was all dependent on me pulling my finger out of my arse and calling him. "That's fine. Where's she off to?"

Pops shrugged. "Night out or something with Campbell and a group of friends, I think she said."

"That's good." My sister and Campbell worked hard, and it was rare for them to have time out by themselves. I was up for any excuse to spend time with Timmy too. He was batshit crazy like his dad, with a bucketload of cuteness that he got from his mum.

"So you wanna tell me what's got you throwing a tantrum?"

"I was not throwing a tantrum." I rolled my eyes, ignoring the edge of a whine in my tone.

Pops's snort told me he thought I was full of it. And I absolutely was, but giving the cantankerous old goat any ammo was not in my best interest.

"You keep telling yourself that, kid." I glanced at him just in time to see him shaking his head in my direction, one of his furry white brows raised high. "This anything to do with where you disappeared to yesterday, returning like a cat that got the cream?"

He followed up with an amused grin, reminding me he rarely let anything slip on by.

I smirked and rolled my eyes at him, reaching for my phone off to the side.

"Hey now, don't you go burying your head in that thing and ignore me." He was silent a beat before he huffed, loudly and filled with humour. "So that's it then. 'Bout bloody time."

"What's that supposed to mean?" I eyed the door, knowing that if I legged it like a teenager, there'd be no catching me, but I thought better of it, grumbling, "Yes, I met up with someone yesterday."

"No shit, Sherlock. I got that much. Spill."

I sighed, immediately lapsing into our true relationship, regressing into a petulant kid as I sat, saying, "The guy's nice. Said he'd call yesterday or today."

When I didn't speak, Pops screwed up his face, his expression telling me where this was going and I was a dick. "Your balls gone and shrivelled up, making it impossible to pick up the damn phone yourself or something?"

I laughed despite my embarrassment at being called out. The man always said it straight. When I'd come out to my family in my late teens, honestly, he'd surprised me the most. My parents had taken it in stride, which I'd expected, my sister too, but my pops I hadn't been quite sure about.

Living and working on a station for most of his life, it wasn't like he was that worldly. But apparently, I knew nothing. When I'd finally told him, he'd simply nodded and told me his best mate Bill was a queer fella, which had also sent my brain spinning. After that, he'd told me to wrap up and not show my arsehole to any good-looking fella who came around asking for a peek.

Needless to say, I'd ended the night trying to forget the whole conversation of Pops talking about my arsehole.

"No," I finally answered.

"You playing hard to get?" he threw out, and I could hear the challenge in his voice.

I shook my head, fully feeling like a kid now.

"So pull your head out of your arse, and if you like the man, do something about it." He narrowed his eyes at me, and I knew what was coming. "James was ill. You shouldn't be paying for that."

There was nothing like Pops going for the gut. There wasn't an edge of sympathy, and certainly no pity in his voice. I was grateful as hell for that. But still, the thought of James, how he'd ended it all, how he'd struggled and I'd been powerless to help him, that shit was hard to deal with. Let alone move on from.

It didn't matter that I deserved to, and I knew, soul deep, that I deserved my slice of love and happiness and goddamn rainbows if I so wanted.

"Thanks, Pops," I mumbled, tilting my lips up, letting him see the truth of my words.

"Good," he said with a nod. "Now let me be. My show's on."

I chuckled, amused as hell the old man had a weird obsession with *The Bachelor*. Picking up my phone, I stood, planning to head outside to quickly check on the progress of some of the cattle who'd be calving soon. As soon as the mobile connected with my hand, it rang, startling me.

Pops snorted. I didn't bother flipping him off or shooting him the stink eye. Instead, my heart raced as I peered at the screen.

Riley.

I willed the massive grin on my face to settle, needing to tone down my reaction so I didn't freak the guy out and come across as the needy loser I possibly was. After a couple of breaths and two more rings, I hit Accept.

"Hey."

"Aiden, hey, it's Riley."

My lips rose into another smile when he told me his name, despite his details lighting up my screen. "Yeah, hey, Riley. How's things?" I asked, impressed my words sounded casual. I reached the door and headed outside, searching for privacy.

"Not too bad, thanks. It's been a night of it. Honestly, I haven't long got back."

Surprise circled me. Did that mean he'd stayed at Pete's?

"I bet you're knackered. Things not go well? Pete's sister?" I added, remembering not to be a selfish dick and that clearly something more serious was likely going on.

A huff of air travelled down the line, his exhaustion evident in that one action. I sucked back even the hint of jealousy. Me being a prick was uncalled for. While I had no idea what had happened, that tired breath validated that his night had been far from fun.

"Not great. Mina, Pete's sister, was due to start chemo tomorrow. She passed out at home yesterday. Took her a while to wake up, so they're keeping her in."

I winced as Riley spoke. I really was an arsehole.

"That's not good," I said, which was putting it mildly. "I didn't know she was ill."

While I wasn't close to Pete, I was surprised I hadn't heard from any of the guys in Outback Boys. They could give knitting circles or whatever a run for their money for how quickly they could share gossip.

Once more, Aiden sighed heavily, and a rustle of something from his end reached my ears. "I didn't know anything until Friday. Pete sort of dropped it on me when I called him out for being quiet and not himself."

"Shit." Understanding hit me. Riley had been with Pete Friday after work. "Do people at your work know?"

"The boss does. He's organised time off."

"That's something."

"Yeah," he said. "So, erm, how're you? Everything okay? Sorry I didn't get a chance to call last night."

A small smile lifted my lips. Despite him supporting Pete last night and clearly being exhausted, he checked up on me and made my stomach flip over in the best of ways.

"Yeah, all good. My day's not been too busy, really. Managed to get on top of a few things I've been putting off." I didn't add that was all with the aim of keeping myself distracted.

"That's good." Riley followed up with a yawn. "Sorry."

I chuckled. "You sound wrecked."

"Pretty much. I best be going. I just wanted to, you know, call you and let you know I had a good time yesterday."

"Yeah?" The need was obvious in my voice. It was loud and clear for him to hear, and I was okay with that.

"Yeah," he said, his voice dipping. "I'd like to do it again sometime soon."

"I'd like that."

"Perhaps next weekend?"

I was nodding and about to say yes when I remembered Timmy. "I'm actually helping Pops look after my nephew Friday and Saturday. We have him overnight."

"You do?"

I laughed at his tone. "Yeah, why? That sounds a bit like disbelief."

He laughed too, saying, "No, no, it's not that. I can just imagine the two of you chasing around after the kid, drumming up more mischief, and that's without even meeting your grandad."

I snorted. "I think you've got him pegged for sure. Me? I'm the sensible one."

"Ha."

"Seriously," I said, amused. "Actually, see for yourself. Why not come and spend the day up here on Saturday? Timmy and I can show you around. You may just be the calming influence he needs." The rightness of the offer settled easily over me.

It didn't matter that it had been only a week since knowing the man. What I saw, I liked. A lot.

There was a beat of silence before Riley responded. "You sure that's okay?" His question was quiet, tentative, but I liked to think there was something more there too.

"Definitely."

"Okay, yeah, sure. I'd like that."

My grin was immediate, responding instinctively to the warmth in his voice. "Brilliant. We'll talk in the week, yeah, and set it up, give you my address?"

"That sounds good. I finish at five every night."

"Talk to you soon then," I said, needing to get off the phone, sure my face would split from the size of my grin. There was a distinct possibility I'd start gushing anytime about now too. "Cheers, Riley."

"Yeah, bye, Aiden."

The call ended, and I stood there grinning like a loon, staring at my phone.

"Thank Christ for that," Pops hollered across the

yard, making me jump. "Thought I'd have to get the doc in to untwist your balls or some shit." A large smile scrunched his wrinkled face, making his eyes barely visible. "Now get that sappy grin off your face and get to it, kid." He waved me off, shaking his head as he ambled back into the house, leaving me smirking and wondering what Pops would have to say about Riley.

Chapter Seven

It had been quiet in the office with no Pete. The week dragged, particularly with the excitement I failed to ignore about seeing Aiden again on Saturday. My attempt at brushing aside the butterflies in my gut and ignoring the swirl of expectation was impossible. And after another chat on the phone with him last night, I'd finally admitted defeat and embraced the feeling.

Aiden was something special. There was no denying that from the moment my eyes had caught on him a couple of weeks back, I'd been drawn to him. For sure, he was good-looking, enough to make me appreciate his cut jaw and honest-to-God pretty eyes.

That attraction had grown twofold since then.

The hours we'd spent together the past couple of weekends, on top of the calls we'd shared every night, meant he was never far from my thoughts.

We were still very much getting to know each other. There was so much left to be shared, and I was okay with that. This wasn't a race. That didn't mean every time we spoke, or I thought about him, I didn't get a stiffy. Combined with that kiss we'd shared and legit, every night this week I'd taken my hand to myself, it had added the fuel I needed to finally push over the edge.

Along with my calls to Aiden, I'd spoken to Pete virtually every day too. Our conversations were a whole different affair. The situation with his sister was a nightmare. Mina's operation had taken place, but they'd had to delay for a couple of days because of her levels or something. They also kept her in the hospital the rest of the week and had no plans to release her just yet, which I thought was rare. Not that I had any experience with cancer treatment or operation recovery times.

And Pete, hell, the guy seemed lost. He was looking after his niece, Georgie, which appeared to be keeping him together, but the strain in his voice hit me every time. It seemed like I was the only friend he had around too, which boggled my mind, as while I liked the guy and definitely had time for him, we didn't know each other that well or even spend a lot of time together outside of work.

Though, with my own complicated history and isolation from my parents, I wasn't surprised that a gay man had little in the way of blood relatives looking out for him. It was that lack of surprise that was seriously crap and a story I'd heard too many times.

I looked at the directions on my phone leading me to Pete's house. Only five minutes more and I'd be at his door, meeting his niece, and hopefully cheering him up—if that was even possible—or more likely just checking he was functioning.

When he'd called earlier during my lunch break, he'd asked me if I minded stopping by after work. I'd agreed immediately, promising to stop by for a couple of hours, and pleased in many ways that he'd asked.

Isolating himself now would be the worst thing he could do, so offering a friendly face and conversation was something I could manage.

A couple more turns, and I pulled up at a brick home on a new estate. The houses were close together, but I imagined from the hills around that from the back, there'd be a great view. After parking,

I made my way to the front door and knocked a couple of times. The padding of little feet followed by a high squeal and mumbled words filtered through, making me smile.

"Don't even try to open that door." A moment later, Pete tugged the door open, a wriggling kid in his arms and a harried look on his face. "Hey, you made it." He smiled and stepped back. "Come on in. Let me let this wriggle butt down before she bounces on her head and gets some sense knocked into her."

"I's not a wiggle worm, Unca Pete." The brown-haired girl's eyes were wide when she looked at her uncle.

"You could have fooled me, kiddo." Pete planted a kiss on Georgie's cheek and let her down. Once her feet were on the ground, she peered up at me.

"You Wiley?"

I grinned. "Yep. You're Georgie, right?"

She bobbed her head enthusiastically. "You wanna look for worms?"

I chuckled and glanced at Pete. A soft smile was on his mouth as he looked down at his niece. "Maybe later. Let the grown-ups get a coffee first, then we'll play a game or something, okay?"

As Pete spoke, I stepped fully into the house,

closing the door behind me and following Pete through the home to the kitchen.

"'Kay," Georgie said before racing off to do who knew what.

Pete let her go without a backward glance and peered over at me. "Coffee?"

I bobbed my head. "That'd be great. Thanks."

He turned and picked up the steaming kettle and poured hot water into a coffee carafe. "Let's head on out back," he said once the sound of high-pitched, tinkling music began from another room. "No chance we can chat with the sound of that kids' TV show." He shook his head, amusement dancing in his tired eyes.

"Need me to grab anything?"

"Milk from the fridge if you want some."

"Black's fine," I answered, following him outside to the small concrete patio area. I glanced around, taking in the hint of a view between the trees. It was a nice little spot. I took a seat at the small wooden table and chairs and eased back. "How've you been?"

Pete's shrug was tight. "As good as could be expected, really. Went to see Mina today." He pressed his lips closed and fell silent.

"She recovering okay?"

He shook his head, a shadow of sorrow sweeping across his features. "Not exactly."

When he didn't continue, I asked, "And what does that mean?"

He swallowed hard before saying, "Do you mind if we talk about something else?"

I shook my head. "Of course not." I started chatting about one of the programs at work and told him about Molly having a hissy fit over something not working out right, and from there, I continued to grasp for topics, doing everything I could do to distract the guy.

When the conversation turned to the outback group, he seemed genuinely surprised when I said I'd definitely be attending the next activity. It was just a morning of surfing, which Aiden had told me about.

"And you want to definitely go again?"

I willed myself to not be defensive at the shock registering in his voice. Schooling my expression and moderating my voice, I answered with a simple "Yeah."

"Oh, okay. Obviously with Mina and everything happening here, I might not be able to make it, so if not, you can always hang around here instead."

I dipped my brows low as I clarified, "Thanks,

but I'll still be going. I've never actually been surfing before," I admitted. "Too many sharks on the west coast for me."

Pete didn't respond as he reached out for his coffee, sending me a smile and a look I couldn't quite decipher. After taking a sip, he said, "That's good that you're going then. I just wasn't sure how comfortable you'd be by yourself, is all."

While his words were kind, there was something in the tone that wasn't quite right. But I imagined the clusterfuck of a week he'd had had a lot to do with his up and down reaction.

"I'll be okay. Plus Aiden will be there."

Pete's brows shot high as soon as Aiden's name passed my lips. "I didn't realise you've been talking to him."

I smiled despite the weirdness of Pete's reaction. "Yeah, we've been talking and texting and spent some time together last week." This was the point where Pete would usually ask for the details and would be OTT in his exuberance. It was his way, and something I'd found entertaining and kinda sweet in the times I'd spoken to him about a rare hook-up. Instead, he nodded and sent me a tight-lipped smile, saying, "That's great. Good for you. After all this time, I'd been wondering what Aiden's type is. Now I know."

I didn't bite, choosing to believe there wasn't bitchiness in his response. Switching the topic, I asked, "And how's Georgie? She's a cute kid."

The look I couldn't describe disappeared from his eyes at the mention of his niece. A small huff of air escaped Pete as a gentle smile curved his lips. "She's amazing. Bloody resilient, you know? She hasn't seen Mina in the hospital. Mina didn't want her to, so I've made sure we've mixed a few fun things with everyday stuff. Mina laid down the law, saying she didn't want her routine screwed up."

"That's great. What's happening about work next week?" Initially, he'd planned to return, expecting to just do short hours while taking Georgie to childcare and caring for his sister. But with his sister not yet released, I wasn't sure if that had changed things for him.

"I spoke to Maxine. She organised for me to work remotely for the next couple of weeks. If there's a briefing I need to be in, I'll join by video. She's been amazing, really."

I nodded, relieved Maxine was showing herself to be a good human being. "I'm just at the end of a phone call if you need anything."

His smile was back, still tired and not quite full, but his gaze softened at my words. "Thanks, mate. I appreciate it." He took another sip of his drink and appeared to study me for a beat. The smile remained on his face as he said, "So Aiden? Dish the dirt, and when are you seeing that delicious specimen again?" A quirked brow followed, and I laughed, expelling a long breath, my chest feeling lighter.

ONCE AGAIN MY SAT NAV DIDN'T LET ME DOWN. IT WAS rare it got so much of a workout, so I was always a little reluctant to trust in the map. All through my late teens, my sister used to take the piss out of me spectacularly due to me still using road maps wherever I went. I chuckled at the memory, pushing aside the pang of sorrow that went hand in hand with thoughts of my sister.

Today, I didn't want to be wallowing in memories still powerful enough to bring me to my knees. Latching onto the good stuff was important, what I needed, and I was determined to do just that as I crawled down the long pot-holed gravel driveway.

A Queenslander was positioned at the top of the small hill. It looked weather-worn, which made it appear charming rather than untidy. While silky oaks lined the long entrance, there were trees in flower dotted around the garden. The jacaranda's distinctive purple was unmistakable, but there were other flowers on trees I had no idea the name of.

A large shed and a collection of outbuildings sat to the side of the property, a good twenty metres or so away. And there, standing in the open double space of the shed doorway with a dog sitting at his feet, tail wagging something fierce, and a boy sitting on a small motorbike, was Aiden. Complete with checked shirt, dark jeans, and work boots, he was every bit my wet dream incarnate. That and the epitome of a sexy cowboy, his Acubra having a lot to do with that look as it perched on his head, set back just enough that his smile wasn't blacked out by the shadow of the brim.

Fuck, he was hot.

As I pulled up to a stop, he took long strides to reach me, shouting something to the boy before pulling my door open. I clambered out immediately, stretched, and then his mouth was on mine.

I startled for a moment before I got my wits about me and leaned into the connection. It was brief, and there wasn't even tongue, but as Aiden pulled away, his smile wide, his eyes on mine, it was the perfect kiss and absolutely the best greeting.

"Hey," he said, just as a boy's loud laughter reached us.

"Ew, kissing is so gross, Uncle Aiden. Yuck."

Aiden snorted, turning his head to look at his nephew. "Yep, you better believe it's gross. No kissing anyone for you until you're at least twenty-five."

I chuckled, and Aiden returned his attention to me, his hand reaching out and holding mine. "Anyone would think you've missed me," I said, shamelessly fishing.

"It's been a long week."

"I know how that feels."

"Come on, let me introduce you to this tearaway. I promised he could have half an hour on his bike."

We walked over to Aiden's nephew. A huge helmet sat on his head, making him look a little like one of those wobbly head statues. Kitted out in padding, he looked the part of a little hellion. "Hey, Timmy, right?" I greeted.

A goofy grin peered out at me through the visor. "Yep. You're..." Timmy screwed up his face as though in deep concentration. His gaze darted to his uncle, eyes wide as he whispered, "I can't remember."

"Riley," Aiden whispered back, his voice light with humour.

"Riley," Timmy said, his smile back on his face. "You can watch me."

"Timmy, manners," Aiden was quick to say, his voice dipped low but no real sternness in his tone.

"Sorry. Can you watch me, please?"

There was no way I could refuse this kid with the cute factor. "I'd love to."

"We're going to jump on the Gator rather than the quad. It's less hairy for you," Aiden said to me, tugging me in the direction of a small ATV. While I knew what a Gator was, I'd never been in one before. I grinned as I stepped up, taking my seat, watching Aiden first head to his nephew.

"Remember to take it easy, especially here till we get to the track, okay?" Once Timmy nodded, Aiden tapped his helmet lightly and helped him start up the tiny bike. "And wait for me."

Timmy bobbed his head once, and I could practically feel his excitement to rev and get going, but he didn't do so until his uncle was at my side, the engine started, and had given the boy the go-ahead.

Then Timmy was off, the two of us following closely behind.

"I put together a small track out the back here for

him to use his bike on," Aiden explained as the dirt mounds with a distinctive pathway came into view. "He keeps his bike here so is always begging to come over to ride. Me and Pops bought it for him for Christmas last year, and he loves the damn thing."

"Wow," I said, my eyes widening as soon as Timmy hit the track and opened the small bike up. He made it all look so easy. "He's killing it."

Aiden snorted as he pulled up at the side of the track underneath a large tree and shut off the engine. I appreciated the shade, having not thought about grabbing my hat out of the car before we headed out.

"He's pretty good. Pisses his dad off that his son seems to be into the bike more than riding horses at the moment," he said jovially.

I laughed. "I bet. Timmy seems to be loving it, though."

"He really does. It's why his dad only grumbles when Timmy's not around." Aiden's grin seemed far from repentant, and I shook my head at him. "So you survived your week okay, then?" he went on to ask.

"Yeah. A little tedious this week. The work was a little monotonous, but I won't complain. Means it was an easy one, and I didn't have to use my brain too much."

"I'm all for enjoying an easy week, for sure."

"Yours been okay?"

"Straightforward. Calving season at the moment, so it's always busy, and most of our stock were heifers, first-timers, so we kept a closer eye on them. Just tidying up the place at the moment, too, preparing for storm season, so trying to get a step ahead and clear out any trees near the fence lines."

"It's never-ending, I bet," I responded as I looked around at what I could see of the property. While Aiden had told me the size, it was hard to visualise without seeing it firsthand. "Where's your property stretch to?"

"Once we get Timmy back and I introduce you to Pops, we'll have a drive round."

"Sounds good," I said, my stomach swooping, knowing how important his pops was to Aiden. From the way he'd greeted me at the car—the kiss in front of his nephew—I kinda figured he was really open about his sexuality, which was great. I was envious of the fact, but it proved difficult to ignore the worry, despite how small it was, when meeting someone's parent, or grandparent in this case. He'd told me about his grandad's reaction, but that didn't stop all the nerves from flitting around. Plus, there was the fact I really liked

Aiden, and I definitely wanted his pops to like me too.

We sat outside for a little over thirty minutes, chatting about our weeks, laughing at a few skids Timmy made and saved before Aiden pulled him aside to stop. Despite a few grumbles, Timmy rode ahead of us back to the house, a plume of dust kicking out behind him. When we reached the shed, he drove straight inside, while Aiden parked the Gator in some shade.

"I'm happy you could come by today," Aiden said when it was just the two of us. His words shot a thrill of happiness to my chest. I liked it a lot that he seemed as eager for my company as I did his. His gaze darted to my mouth, and anticipation swirled around me. The tension between us sparked to life, the need for his mouth on mine a steady pulse beating loud and fierce in tune with my heart.

"Me too," I said quietly, leaning closer towards him in clear invitation.

The quirk of his lips followed by the barest wetting of his bottom lip had my focus zeroing in on his mouth. He leaned closer, and my eyes slid shut at the contact of his mouth on mine. Our lips brushed, moved, and opened. A tentative dip of the tongue, followed by another. The contact sent a shiver down my spine and heat to my cock.

Just as my hand made contact with his stubbled jaw, the words "And so it begins. Boy, let the man be so he can take a breath already" had the two of us jarring apart.

Wide-eyed, I looked over Aiden's shoulder, my gaze settling on an old man standing in the open doorway of the house.

"Shit, sorry." Aiden's apology had my eyes darting back to his. "The old man just doesn't have a clue about perfect timing," he continued, this time much louder, and his words clearly intended for his grandad. "He's a good guy. You'll get used to him," he said, sending me a reassuring smile.

I worked hard to ignore the heat in my cheeks from being caught making out, feeling once more like a teenager. It was becoming something of a habit, blundering and behaving like I hadn't shared a kiss before. Admittedly, I never had with someone as sexy or... hell, anyone like Aiden before.

"We'll finish this up later," he said, shooting me a wink and standing. "Pops," he called out, looking at his grandfather, "behave. I'll go and sort Timmy."

My ears tuned in to the sound of movement in the shed, and a sliver of guilt edged towards my gut that we'd simply left a six-year-old to fend for himself. Though the casual stroll from Aiden didn't scream urgency, so I pushed my discomfort aside and made my way towards Aiden's grandad.

"G'day. Name's Riley," I greeted, taking his hand in mine for a shake. I wasn't surprised by the strength of his grip, despite his worn and wrinkled body.

His steady gaze met mine, bright blue orbs taking me in. "Warren, but you can call me Pops." A crooked smile followed. "Little Timmy go okay?"

I nodded, not quite sure what to do with the warmth in my chest from Warren's easy acceptance, nor his invite for me to call him Pops. "He sure did. Little hellraiser."

Warren snorted, the action making me smile, as it reminded me of his grandson. "He is that. Aiden and I are on a mission to make the kid a petrol head, just to piss his dad off." He laughed loudly, the sound rich and deep, and I joined in with a quieter chuckle.

"Yeah, Aiden did say something about that."

"Come on in. We'll sit out back. View's better, and there's a good breeze too. You can take the drinks out."

I didn't hesitate to do as instructed, following

Warren's orders, making coffee and a jug of juice. By the time I had three steaming mugs outside, three glasses, a plastic tumbler, and the jug rattling with ice cubes as they floated in the juice, Aiden joined us, his nephew not far behind him talking animatedly about one of his saves.

We spent the afternoon laughing while Warren regaled us with tales of Aiden when he was a kid and a teen. On top of that, we played soccer with Timmy, and when Aiden showed me around his property once more in the Gator truck, just the two of us this time, our touches became more insistent, our tender kisses more heated.

By the time we pulled back up at the house, it was late afternoon. The sun still beat down on us, heating my skin, but Aiden was 100 percent responsible for my flushed cheeks and my reluctance to step out of the small truck.

"You need a minute?" He side-eyed me, his lips twitching while he not so subtly adjusted his jeans.

With desire riding me from when he'd pulled up behind a clump of trees before returning to the shed, his hand moving to my groin and stroking over my own denim-covered cock, the words spilled out of me: "I need a whole night." Roughness filled my words, the truth of them obvious.

I didn't do upfront. Didn't make bold declarations. And I definitely didn't usually make a statement that I wanted to spend the whole night with a guy. But that was the difference. Aiden wasn't any guy.

For two weeks, we'd spent hours talking and spending time with one another. It was fast, and I was surprisingly more than okay with that.

I'd be even better if he agreed to come home with me.

Aiden angled his head to face me. Heat danced in the depths of his eyes. My mouth went dry at that one look. "I'll pack a bag. Emily is due soon, so Pops will be fine for the thirty minutes or so."

I searched his gaze, not quite sure what I was looking for. Certainty, perhaps. A reassurance that he was as much into me as I was into him. But I didn't find either in his eyes. Instead, my breath caught when he said, "It took me a minute to understand I wanted to get to know you. It took maybe an hour to figure that *how* I wanted to get to know you was as more than friends." He stopped speaking as he peered at me, eyes unwavering as they connected with my own. "And it took just one bounce of a possessed bowling ball and having you look at me the way you do for me to know I want to see where this goes."

I nodded, my breathing a little heavier than when he'd first started speaking. "Tonight I'd like that to be with me, at home, in my bed."

"Deal," he said, dotting a kiss on my mouth and pulling away immediately. "If we move fast, I think we can be out of here in ten minutes. I'll text Emily as well, letting her know I'm not going to be here so she doesn't drag her feet."

It didn't take long for him to speak to his pops, grab a pair of boxers and a toothbrush, reassure his nephew he could have a sleepover again soon, and let Warren know he'd be home by nine and make him promise to call if there were any problems.

We left in a haze of need and tension as I said a slightly awkward goodbye to Aiden's grandad, who was far from subtle with his knowing grin and a reminder to wrap up. The same tension eased barely forty minutes into the journey when we started talking about places we'd visited inside and outside Australia.

I drove, letting Aiden know I'd bring him back tomorrow. The whole trip down the Bruce Highway, his hand didn't leave the back of my neck. He alternated with stroking the skin, giving light massage-like squeezes, and scraping his nails across my scalp. Originally when he'd placed his palm there rather than my thigh, I'd been relieved, sure it meant I'd calm my erection down. That didn't happen at all. Not with the shift between relaxing strokes to subtle caresses. And while the tension had simmered to a dull throb between us, I ached in the best of ways.

By the time we pulled up outside of my place, I was strung out. The last fifteen minutes of the journey were agony when I knew how close I was to home and getting my hands and mouth on the man. He made my heart beat wildly in my chest.

The door was barely closed before we pressed against each other. Our mouths met with an urgency that threatened to unravel me, and by the time I led Aiden to my bedroom, both of our T-shirts were off, shoes kicked off, and our jeans were unbuckled.

My hands were down his boxers, caressing and stroking, while our kisses turned more urgent, more possessive. Heat raced along every cell in my body, desire unfurling low in my gut and making my balls tighten.

"Naked," I mumbled against his mouth when I forced myself to take a breath. We needed to slow down. I wanted to savour every moment Aiden gave me.

He eased away, his lips swollen, eyelids heavy, and when he tugged down his jeans and boxers, his cock sprung free, jutting proudly. A bead of precum caught my attention, making it impossible to look away as I shoved off the rest of my clothes.

His length bobbed under my fixed gaze, and Aiden spoke, his tone deep, breathy, and sounding as close to the edge as I was when he said, "You keep looking at my cock like that...." He trailed off, and I flashed a glance his way.

Without a word, I was before him and easing him back to my mattress. When his knees hit the edge, he sat, thighs parting for me when I sank down to my knees.

"Fuck." The single word from him was strained.

I watched his face closely when I ran my hands up his thighs, never recalling a time before I'd acted like this with a man. The difference was clear, significant.

Without a doubt I knew Aiden wanted me as much as I wanted, *needed* him. That right there was a heady thing and threw all my inhibitions right out the window.

Anticipation clawed at me, making my dick throb as I licked my bottom lip, preparing to taste him. Horny didn't even come close to describing how Aiden made me feel.

I didn't touch him immediately. Instead, I took my fill, soaked in the look of him, appreciating the way his cock bobbed, the way the veins were perfectly positioned to guide my tongue along.

Just as Aden said a breathy "Riley," I ran my tongue over his length, exploring the softness of his skin that contrasted perfectly with the steel of his cock. Pulling back, I trailed my tongue around the head, dipping my tongue and finally tasting him.

Aiden's throaty moan had my gaze flicking up. The need in his eyes spurred me on as I opened wide, went deep, and feasted on him.

His moan turned into a grunt that turned into mumbled words of lust. Each eager praise, each cry for more, I welcomed, wanting so desperately to show him exactly how incredible he was and how he made me feel.

I peered up at him once more as I came up for air, moving my hand to his length, stroking. Aiden's heat-filled eyes stared back at me, and he tugged his bottom lip into his mouth.

"Suck me harder," he grunted, his unwavering glance fierce, desperate.

I smirked, loving how close he was to unravelling. With my one hand gripping the base, I inhaled through my nose and pushed deep, sucking fiercely.

His grunts spurred me on, his hands finding my head, my face, caressing, stroking. Each touch and desperate plea urged me to blow his mind. Forcing all of the air out of my lungs, I pushed forwards. It had the desired effect. His cock hit the back of my throat. Desire, heat, delicious waves of need rolled through my limbs. My body was on fire. My speeding pulse pounded in my ears. I held a moment before easing back, gasping for breath.

Aiden's firm hand on my cheeks surprised me, jerking my attention his way.

"No more," he said, his chest rising and falling rapidly. "I want you inside me when I come."

My mouth was on him in an instant, our mouths sliding against each other. It was difficult to think, to hold on to rational thought. Need like I'd never known before threatened to buckle my knees and have me explode before my poor dick saw any action.

Pulling back a little abruptly, I gasped for breath. I'd managed to hoist myself up and was straddling him.

"You okay?" he asked, concern in his voice and tenderness in his eyes.

"Yeah. Just need to slow down," I admitted with a shrug, new heat hitting my cheeks.

He bobbed his head, his lips curving upwards. "Slowing down is good." He angled a look behind him. "Bed?"

I grinned and dotted a peck to his mouth before pulling back. "Yeah, let's get comfortable and let me grab some supplies." My eyes widened when I realised I'd sucked him off without protection. Shit, I never did that. In my defence, I hadn't had sex with anyone beyond a one-night stand in years, making it absolutely imperative I protected myself.

"What's wrong?" Aiden asked, stopping me from moving.

I sat a little awkwardly on his lap before just coming out with it. Hell, if I couldn't talk about this, I shouldn't be sucking him off and hopefully having my dick in his arse. "I usually insist on a condom."

His brows shot up, and I saw immediate understanding register on his face. "Good. Me too. Though it's been some time," he said, piquing my curiosity enough for me to store that titbit away for when we reached the point of discussing our pasts. "And on that note, I haven't been sexually active for over a couple of years now. Before then, I had a health check. Everything was negative."

Two years. My heart lurched. I knew immediately he was referring to the boyfriend who'd died. It wasn't something we'd discussed, and I had no intention of ever bringing up the gossip shared with me by the Outback Boys.

"It's rare for me," I felt compelled to say. Not only because it was the truth, but it just felt like the right thing to share. "My last check was six months ago. All negative, and no one since." When he smiled, my heart lurched for a whole different reason, knowing oversharing was the right thing to do.

I hoped we were building something here. It sure felt like it, and while sex was most definitely about to happen, the rest we could navigate at a speed that suited us too. I didn't want to be governed by time-lines, and I thought Aiden would happily agree.

"Supplies?" He squeezed the globes of my butt when he spoke, and my hips jerked, our dicks pressing against each other. I sighed at the contact, wanting as much of his body pressed against mine as possible.

With one last kiss, I grinned and then angled off him, watching Aiden scoot back while I went to the bedside drawers.

As he moved, his muscles shifted, looking so

damn lickable. The action, the man's comfort in his own skin, pulled me up short.

I was butt naked in front of this sexy-as-hell man, yet my usual self-consciousness didn't kick in. Aiden never gave it the chance to. Not with the way his eyes ate me up. Not with how his hands roamed my soft flesh when we'd stumbled through the house to get to my bedroom.

I swiped a condom and a bottle of lube with renewed focus, and I was on him.

My hands were everywhere, my mouth tracing a similar trail as I got my fill of the man who made my heart bounce so hard that at any moment I was sure it would fly right out of my chest. The whole time his own lips, his own hands travelled over my skin. Each caress, each lick sent wave after wave of desire flowing through me, dragging me under, leaving me gasping for breath. And with lungs full of air, slow was no longer within my grasp as I urged Aiden onto his hands and knees.

"You're so incredible," I said on a wisp of a breath as I prepared him, encouraging him to ride my fingers to make sure he was ready.

Aiden was incoherent, unable to finish his words, let alone a sentence, as his body shook, sweat glistening on his skin.

"You ready for me?" I asked.

"God, yes."

I grinned and, with shaking hands, sheathed myself and pressed against him, whispering gentle encouragement until my own words escaped me. Words bled into each other, heat surrounded me, and my brain fogged despite the energy and hunger zipping along my body.

Aiden was strength and warmth. He met each thrust with a push and cry for more. He was perfection in his needy whimpers that wrapped around me soul deep, taking me by surprise. The man before me was so much more than I expected.

He let go, released in my hand as I followed the climb and flew. Flying high and struggling to feel my body, I pressed against him, leaning over, letting my weight rest on him. At his movement, I glanced up to see Aiden turning his head, seeking me out.

A flutter of affection took flight in my chest, and I found the energy to smile and lean forwards so I could press my lips against his. Our breaths were heavy as we pulled away, and I eased out.

Free to collapse, I did so to his side, my arm immediately scooping around his chest and tugging Aiden towards me. He came willingly, his heart pounding under my hand.

"That was..." I searched for the right word, struggling to say the right thing without sounding like a sexed-hazed fool, but since I was, I went with "...incredible. Seriously amazing." My lips found purchase on the side of his neck. He sighed at the touch, and my like for the man grew with each shaky breath he took.

After a few beats of steadying our inhales and exhales, Aiden nodded and turned his head to look back at me. "It was," he said, his eyes full of sleep and what I thought was contentment. The smile that lit his face screamed of satisfaction. I mirrored it, wanting him to see just how honest my words were.

"Shower, then food?"

He flopped his head on the pillow with a disgruntled moan.

Laughing, I said, "Come on. Hose down, then I'll get us fed."

A quick glance back at me told me he was mulling over my offer. "Only if we can have takeout. I never get the chance to have takeout at home. Live too far from anywhere for the food not to be cold by the time I get it home."

"Oh... no Uber Eats up your way, then, huh? Sucks. And I can totally make your night by making that happen."

"You've already made my night." His words were quiet and said with an intensity that surprised me, enough to catch my breath. He turned fully to face me, scrunching his nose up during the move and wincing, completely breaking the spell his words put me under. "Found the wet spot."

I laughed loudly, the sound abrupt and sudden and rattling me with genuine amusement. "We'll order takeout, and then I'll change the bed sheets," I offered, enjoying the humour while snatching his earlier words and tucking them away for me to mull over another time.

"A real gentleman, huh?"

I snorted. "Always."

Chapter Eight

AIDEN

THE PAST COUPLE OF WEEKS HAD BEEN BOTH BUSY AND spectacular.

Life went on as usual on the property. My days were filled with the normal tasks of checking the calving cows, assisting with a couple of pain in the arse calves who struggled to enter the world, and herding the cattle from the Rosebud grazing paddock to Ted's paddock. I'd be moving them again on Monday. This time to the Blouse Barn paddock. I had a couple of workhands who came to help on such days, both on horses while I stuck with my quad.

The guys soon got used to the names assigned to the paddocks too. And when I'd discovered Jerry, one of the guys who helped out a few hours a week, had since binged *Schitt's Creek* to "see what all the fuss was about," to say that I was amused was an understatement.

It was kinda neat that I was opening up the world of straight men, one TV episode at a time.

But it wasn't that nothing out of the ordinary had happened on the property that made the past couple of weeks so great. Nope. That was all to do with Riley.

The man was under my skin in the best of ways.

For days after that first night together, I'd felt the burn with every step I took. The wince was easy to ignore when with every ache of discomfort, the memory of him buried deep inside me, the ghost of his hands and his mouth all over me, hit me full force. The smile then came easily, to the point that Pops was worried I was becoming "simple."

After trying once more to remind him of the importance of word selection and not to be a derogatory old man—right alongside his usual response of "Yeah, I'll get right on that"—I'd reassured him I was happy. Simple as that.

There was little doubt he was as surprised as I was with me admitting that aloud.

I'd managed to spend the whole following weekend with Riley. He'd come by the Friday night after work, "helped" with some jobs on Saturday, which was kind of endearing, and slept over both nights.

Once he'd realised Pops's room was at the opposite end of the house, he'd relaxed some and had happily obliged in blowing my mind. It seemed his new mission was to see just how incoherent he could make me.

Last night was the first time I'd stayed over at his place. Despite him living in suburbia, it was still the hinterland, so it wasn't as close or claustrophobic as if he lived in a big town or city. He had a nice set-up going, and on the plus side, he had a king-size bed. It made getting up at six this morning to get to the beach at seven a challenge.

The familiarity of being wrapped up in Riley was my new favourite thing, and I grumbled relentlessly as he practically dragged me out of bed.

"You're usually up well before this time in the morning," he said at my side as we pulled up into a parking space.

I shrugged. "But that's when I'm alone in bed." I threw him a salacious grin, earning me a chuckle. His eyes were bright, his attention all mine as I hauled him in for a kiss. That he came willingly flooded me with warmth. He pulled away, nudging me to grab my things before he exited the car.

Contentment, I thought, my gaze fixed on his shorts-clad arse, was a foreign concept, which was all levels of sad if I allowed myself to overthink it, but beyond happy times as a child, I didn't think I'd felt so at peace.

I knew most of that was to do with my headspace and how lucky I was to have a job I loved. But I wasn't naïve enough to not recognise that Riley being in my life, bringing with him a calm, a rightness, had something to do with it too. Plus, there was that arse that I was sure he stuck out just a little further as he bent to pick something up from the floor. I liked to think he knew I had my eyes on him.

As I allowed myself to consider how grateful I was, my mind slipped to James.

Life with James… well, it had never been this, never been easy. Passionate? Sure. Intense? Definitely. The truth was, he'd been broken, his illness destroying him, and in the end, I didn't have the power or the energy to keep trying to fix him. It had been impossible to do such a thing, but I'd tried for so damn long.

"If you've changed your mind, we can go have a

big breakfast instead," Riley called from the open boot of his car, startling me.

"I thought you were excited to give surfing a try?" As I stepped out of the car, I stretched and took in the view before glancing over at Riley. I hoped he was joking. When my gaze met his and I didn't see terror in their depths, I smiled, relieved. "You'll do fine. We'll make dicks of ourselves together."

One of his brows quirked high, and he tilted his head. "You sure you're not trying to make me feel better by pretending you're shit at surfing?"

I chuckled and made my way over to him. "You forget I'm from Alice. I'm an outback boy through and through. I don't think the guys who started the group out there a few years back had any intention of surfing. And since I was sixteen when I first saw the ocean... yeah, this activity does not come naturally to me at all."

"That blows my mind," Riley responded as he threw his wallet and phone in the boot of his car. I did the same and grabbed our towels and rash vests. "Not seeing the ocean till you were that age."

I shrugged and challenged, "When was the first time you saw red dirt?"

With a roll of his eyes, he smirked. "Okay, wise guy, point taken." Riley glanced behind us, where our group was already congregating. The shift in his stance was subtle, but I saw it.

"All okay?"

His gaze connected with mine, and he huffed out a small laugh. "Yeah, I just...."

"What?" I pressed, not sure what had changed.

"I don't know these guys. Yeah, I spent a weekend and chatted, and that's fine, but now we're here together...." His brows dipped low. "Is that weird?"

Understanding rippled in my mind. Without a doubt I expected a few looks, maybe a few comments, but the group was really a bunch of good blokes. For sure, the gossips of the group would get their fill, and I didn't care about any of it. "Weird? No." I shook my head. "You seemed to get on well with a couple of the guys when you came before. Mark and Trey, right?" I didn't need to ask, as I'd barely kept my eyes off Riley all weekend. It was his own fault for being so damn sweet and captivating with his smiles and awkwardness. "And you said Pete's coming, right?"

"Yeah, he is, and I sound ridiculous. Ignore me." He rolled his eyes, and I knew the gesture was directed at himself.

"You don't sound ridiculous. Just continue to be your handsome self."

He snorted. "Yeah, right. Come on. Let's do this."

I put my hand in his without a word and squeezed, holding tight, reassuring him that I was exactly where I wanted to be. With him.

Once we headed over to the group, almost everyone took the fact that we arrived hand in hand in their stride. There were a couple of second glances, sure, but each look directed our way was friendly and teamed with a smile.

That I was with Riley would be noted by the group. And that wasn't my arrogance talking. The fact was in the time since I'd moved and joined the Sunshine Coast chapter of Outback Boys, I'd always been friendly, sure, made an effort to support everyone with their activities, but beyond Frank, I pretty much kept to myself.

While I wouldn't exactly say I'd been standoffish, I hadn't been overly open or keen to form a friendship beyond these occasional meetups. The reality was, since James, I'd been emotionally spent, and joining the group to keep myself sane had been as far as I could push it.

A quick glance to my side and the reassuring warmth of Riley's hand in mine made everything different, and, fuck, I was happy about that.

Before long, we were armed with boards and

paddling over the small waves. I could handle this bit, and looking over to my right and seeing Riley scooping his hands through the water, a smile on his face, it seemed he was both coping and enjoying it too.

He glanced at me as we made it over the next small wave, this one sending me a face full of spray. His laughter was loud. My grin was immediate at the sound and the happy look he sent my way.

"The instructor said we should aim to go out a bit further," I called. The wind wasn't too bad, so I didn't have to shout.

Riley bobbed his head, and we carried on.

About twenty of us were out today, a good crowd, which was expected when it was a local activity and not an overnighter.

Pete hadn't shown up. Concern had shone in Riley's eyes when he'd realised as much. Even though I wanted Riley all to myself, I pulled my head out of my arse and suggested he call the guy to check in with him, hoping that whatever was going on would at least ease Riley's worry.

Before he did just that, Frank let us know Pete had texted him to say he had childcare issues, which meant that Riley was able to relax enough to enjoy himself. For a while there, I'd worried Riley felt guilty and would skip the session. I felt like a prick for being so selfish, but it was difficult knowing Riley's attention wasn't mine alone. I had to come to grips with the fact that now I'd finally opened myself to him, it didn't mean I could monopolise all his time.

With the sun beating down on us, the gentle waves bobbing us up and down and creating a welcoming, almost relaxing sound, I refocused on enjoying the moment with Riley. We reached a calm in the ocean, and I pushed myself up to sit, legs spread either side of the board. Riley followed suit, wobbling a little.

"No taking the piss too harshly when I wipe out," he said next to me, his smile letting me know he wouldn't mind so much if I did, though.

I laughed. "You really don't believe me, huh, about not having mad surfing skills?"

When his gaze roamed over my rash-vest-covered chest, his eyes heating, my dick twinged, having a complete mind of its own where Riley was concerned. "I'll wait to see with my own eyes," he said.

I shook my head at him. "That's just cruel... eagerly waiting to see me face-plant in the water," I said with a chuckle. "You think you know someone."

Riley snorted. "You'll be right. Just think, you can sit back and enjoy the moment I attempt to clamber my fat arse up onto this board."

There was jest in his voice, but beneath that, I knew there was some genuine anxiety. He'd mentioned a few times about his fitness levels and his size. While I was all for Riley getting fitter, for the important reason of living a healthy, longer life, his size, his soft edges, the areas he seemed concerned about, those I simply found attractive on him.

"Your arse is fucking perfect." I lifted a brow at him, daring him to challenge me. When he pressed his lips together and a sliver of pink crawled across his cheeks, I exhaled in relief, sure my words had made their mark. "You're sexy as hell, Riley. I wouldn't want you any other way than you are now." My gaze didn't waver as I spoke, and when he didn't respond, my lips curled upwards when I said, "That doesn't mean I won't take great joy in watching your said arse clamber up on the board, though."

A smile spread across his lips, but before he could respond, I peered out at the building wave.

"Looks like I'll get my chance to do just that. This one's yours, Riley."

Horror danced across his features for a moment before he smoothed his expression, glanced at the wave, then nodded in my direction. "Shit, I just turn and paddle, right?"

"Yeah, go, go, go," I shouted to him with a laugh. "Paddle, paddle, paddle!"

He did just that, paddling hard, long, and sure strokes as the wave caught up.

"Pop up!" I hollered.

I watched as his shoulders came off the surface and both feet made purchase with the board. My brows shot up, impressed as hell. I would have loved to have seen his expression at that moment.

For a few brilliant moments, he stayed on his feet, legit riding the wave before slamming down like a felled tree. A loud scream joined the moment, and a raucous laugh burst out of me at his windmilling arms, finished off with a big splash. His head bobbed to the surface a moment later.

Riley came up spluttering as he inhaled. His gaze searched me out. And when our eyes caught, my breath rushed out of me at the joy painted on his face. Bright wide eyes peered over at me, and the grin he wore was the biggest I'd ever seen. He punched the air. "Woo-hoo! Holy shit, did you see that?"

I laughed loudly, pleasure at his reaction racing across my skin, leaving warmth in its wake. Riley was stunning like this, so happy and open. "Yes!" I shouted. "You nailed it!"

Smiling, Riley nodded, looking thoroughly pleased with himself, his gaze moving to my side. "This one's yours!" he called.

A quick glance over my shoulder told me he was right. A decent-sized wave was building. I grinned, despite knowing with 100 percent surety I would wipe out immediately. But I didn't give a toss. The high of Riley's win was a heady thing, and even though I was awful at surfing, the rush of being pushed along with the wave was still pretty cool.

I paddled with long arms, hearing Riley's loud encouragements through the growing sound of the wave. I grinned, ignoring the spray on my face, embracing his support and enthusiasm. My arms worked overtime until the board lifted with the force of the wave, telling me it was time to pop up.

I did so immediately, both feet finding purchase. With my knees bent, I wobbled, feeling the bounce of the wave under my feet. The wave shifted, and I was still crouched low, unable to get my balance enough to stand upright. Another bounce, and my eyes widened, my gaze immediately finding Riley's.

His laughter was enough to warn me of the inevitable.

I tipped, the world tilted, and I hit the water. With my head fully submerged, I paddled up, hands held high to make sure the board didn't smack into my head, which had happened a time or two. Sunlight hit me along with fresh air, and I gulped in a huge breath.

I shook my head and swept a hand over my face, finally opening my eyes. Riley was a few metres to my right, his loud laughter still filling the space between us.

He tried three times to speak, each time unsuccessfully as I paddled over to him. By the time I reached his side, my grin was stretched wide, and he was no longer clutching his stomach. Instead, quieter chuckles bubbled to the surface, and he wiped what were clearly tears from his eyes.

I sat up and splashed him, the seawater hitting its mark and spraying over his face. As he wiped his face again, he said, "Thank you." He wheezed for breath as he continued, saying, "Seriously, I can't remember a time I laughed so hard."

"Hey," I said, amusement colouring that one word, "it wasn't that funny."

Riley was shaking his head before I finished speaking. "No, it really was. Shit, how did you do that?"

I couldn't stop my chuckles from spilling out as fresh tears leaked from his eyes, his laughter renewing. "Do what?"

He shook his head, clearly trying to calm himself down enough to speak. He took a fortifying breath and expelled it, albeit a little shakily. "That..." He snickered. "You bounced like a kangaroo on acid. Like, literally did this weird bounce, hopping thing." His chortles were back as he pressed against his chest. "Oh my God, I think I'm going to have a heart attack. Can laughing too much kill a man?"

"It just might if you carry on," I said, shoving him off the board so he landed with a loud splash in the water. His laughter joined mine when he came up to the surface. He hung on to the board, staring up and over at me. His laughter had calmed some, but nothing but amused pleasure lit his features.

"It was the best thing ever. I need to find a way to video that shit if that's what you do all the time." He reached over to me, still bobbing in the water, one hand on his board, the other finding purchase on my thigh.

The way he peered up at me did something pretty spectacular to my heart. It flipped and dipped and dived before leaping or some shit. "Shift out the way a minute," I instructed, no longer wanting so much distance between us.

He edged back, and I flipped off my board, reaching for him immediately.

When my hand drifted under his arm and I snagged his back, I moved forwards while pulling him closer. At the closeness, his laughter died down, but that perfect smile still played on his lips.

Without speaking, I pressed my mouth against his. Ignoring the seawater was easy, especially when he dipped his tongue past my lips, lightly gliding it against my own. Our lips brushed in synch, the pressure just right, even with our slightly dubious buoyancy. Somehow I managed to force myself closer, clinging to him for dear life, not wanting to miss a moment with his mouth against mine.

His legs came up, tangling around my waist, and I groaned in appreciation as his fabric-covered cock brushed against mine. He jerked forwards, the contact exquisite, though what I wouldn't give to have him exposed and his flesh in my hand.

Riley's mouth eased out of the kiss and away a fraction. He darted his eyes around to the sides and behind me before returning his gaze to mine. "You know, like this, I'm sure we could get each other off.

No one's close." His breathy suggestion was filled with a need that matched my own.

I glanced over his shoulder and to the sides.

The closest people to us were Trey and Mark, a good thirty metres away. Immediately, I removed my hand from his back and slipped it down the front of his shorts.

Riley groaned. "I'll take that as a yes, that you're down for it," he said with a chuckle and ended on a groan when I squeezed a little, my hand moving quickly.

With his legs still wrapped around my waist, keeping us close, he moved his free hand to my shorts. "I need you to slip them down a bit," he said breathily.

I groaned, releasing him, but we managed to get full access to each other's cocks between the two of us.

My gaze fixed on Riley's as I took fast, measured strokes, trying my hardest to concentrate on tipping him over the edge while not losing myself in his touch. And not forgetting to tread water and getting a mouthful of ocean.

His hand was firm, sure, and glided over me perfectly.

My balls tingled, and I clamped my bottom lip between my teeth, forcing myself to not shout out.

At the move, Riley's gaze travelled to my mouth, his eyes sparking with heat, his hand picking up speed.

"Fuck," he murmured.

"I need your mouth," I begged, desperate for his tongue, desperate for the additional connection. He gave it to me immediately.

Within seconds of his tongue brushing against mine, his hand working me over, stars danced behind my closed lids. My balls tightened to the point of my body becoming taut, while somehow, I managed to remember to keep my hand pumping.

I groaned into the kiss, body shuddering as I came so hard it was only Riley's hold on me that kept me afloat and not inhaling seawater.

He came a moment later, his tongue in my mouth and me catching his whimpers. We eased away, both gasping for breath, our hands on each other's flaccid cocks. Tingles continued to dance across my skin, zip around my body, and my energy was completely drained.

"Holy shit," I whispered with a small laugh, not yet letting my eyes dart around to double-check, albeit a little late, to make sure no one had closed in on us in the rolling waves.

Eyes at half-mast, Riley looked as spent as I did. A flush painted his cheeks, and like this, he looked so sexy. He chuckled and eased his hand out of my shorts. Reluctantly I did the same, and we hitched our shorts up to cover our arses.

"You good?"

I bobbed my head. "Absolutely."

He smiled at my answer. "You think we were obvious?"

This time I peered around. Relief steadied my heart, seeing we were alone. A few guys bobbed in the water in the distance, but it would have taken a loud holler for them to hear us. The boards, which we still clung to, floated either side of us, offering us some shelter from curious glances. "No one's around," I offered, adding, "Obvious?" I shrugged, since it was abundantly clear we'd been making out. Though I didn't expect anyone would think we'd get so carried away and start jacking each other off. "Does it matter that I don't give a shit?"

Riley smirked. "Does it matter that I have zero regrets?" he fired back before leaning in and pressing his mouth to mine. He edged back, preventing me from taking the kiss deeper. My grumble made him laugh. "I'm knackered."

With a laugh, I nodded in agreement. "Yeah, perhaps we should have attempted a few more waves first." I glanced out at the ocean. There were still decent sets coming in. All fairly small, about three or four feet, so perfect for us to keep playing and practicing in. "Come on. I'm sure you've not had enough of seeing me get wiped out yet."

Riley pulled himself on to his board. "True, especially if you do more of those kangaroo-on-acid bounces."

I flipped him off. "Fuck off," I shouted, a huge grin on my face. Throwing me a wink, he didn't stop paddling out, leading the way to the building waves.

I followed him happily, more than aware that I'd do the same out of the waves too.

Chapter Nine

THE DATE HIT ME HARD. EVEN THOUGH IT WASN'T A surprise and I knew exactly what day and month it was, it didn't stop the punch of pain.

Fifteen years on, and it hadn't gotten easier. While I'd forced myself to accept my life as it was, attempted to make peace with my past, the churning guilt, the powerful hit of sadness remained true. It was the only day I allowed myself to truly feel it.

Aiden's text telling me he missed me made me smile despite my aching heart. When not waking up beside him, it was the best alternative I had—opening my eyes to one of his texts.

My finger hovered around the Call button. It would be good to hear his voice, maybe even share the significance of the day with him. Instead, I shot him a text back, returning his sentiment, and pocketed my phone.

Today I'd allow myself to wallow. While I would tell Aiden about my sister, the crash, my involvement, it wasn't the right moment. I didn't want his sympathy, his pity, or even his understanding—or maybe his disappointment. Not today.

A quick glance at the time told me it was still too early to call Perth with the time difference. I'd give it a few hours and try as I did every year. The nursing staff and care workers at the facility were pretty amazing and I knew risked a lot to give me the titbits of information that they did, and selfishly, I'd continue to call every year on this day, as well as every month just to know my sister was still breathing.

Miracles weren't real. I never expected to call up and be told Tanya had healed, that she was fully cognizant. For six months she'd been in intensive care after the accident. And when she'd finally woken from a medically induced coma during that time, my parents had decided they didn't have the time or resources to care for her at home, and instead, Tanya had been placed in a long-term nursing home.

It had been a hell of a blow. But my voice had

been squashed the moment the crash had happened. Though truthfully, it had been muted the moment I'd come out.

With my sister at the forefront of my mind, I headed to work, trying to grasp on to happier times when we were kids. There were lots of them, and I was grateful for every single memory. As I pulled up at work, I caught a glimpse of Pete's car, the sight making me smile and offering a welcome distraction.

I hadn't seen him for a couple of weeks, and while we spoke a lot, it was no longer every day. His sister showed some positive signs of recovery since her surgery, and it no longer seemed as though Pete was hanging on by a thread while he balanced caring for her and his niece.

I was happy for them all, desperately so. Over the weeks since Pete had first confided in me about his sister's illness, our friendship had naturally grown, to the point where I could easily shoot him a text to see how he was doing and counted him as a friend without reservations.

After the walk upstairs to the office floor, I smiled, allowing myself the moment of grace that I wasn't gasping for breath after the climb. Religiously I'd used the staircase and felt better for it. The whole combination of that, my regular beach walks, a new friendship, and the significant impact of having Aiden in my life created changes I was grateful for. Ones I'd never anticipated.

The thought sent a flicker of happiness to swirl in my stomach that I refused to extinguish despite knowing that Tanya would never have the same opportunities. Tonight I'd think more about that when it was just me, my thoughts, and my photo album.

"Hey," I said with a grin as soon as I spotted Pete. He surprised me by standing and giving me a hug. My eyes widened at the greeting, but I hugged him back. "All okay?" I asked when he pulled away. Even though he'd grinned back, I was all too familiar with the ease of disguising hurt.

"Yeah," he said, "Just came in to negotiate my time."

My brows dipped. "You need more time off?" Concern lit my words, and I took a moment to rake my eyes over the man. Darkness coloured the space beneath his eyes, and while his hair was styled as it usually was, he appeared a little dishevelled.

While he seemed more together than the last few times I'd seen him, which was a relief, under-standably, he wasn't his relaxed, fun-loving self.

"Not time off as much as the hours to match the childcare place, you know? They do early mornings and stay open till six, but I really think Georgie needs as much time with Mina as possible. She's struggling too much not seeing her mum." I didn't miss the hard swallow or the way he flicked away his gaze when he said those last words. They slammed into me, adding another thick layer of sadness on my chest.

I didn't comment, didn't question his words. Everything about Pete's tone and his body language screamed for me to let him be. I settled on "Okay, that should work, right? Later starts, early finishes?"

Gratitude shone in his eyes as his gaze reconnected with mine. "Yeah, I hope so. I have a meeting at nine thirty with HR. Everyone's amazing, understanding, you know?"

I bobbed my head and kept my hands to myself, despite the need to reach out and grasp his arm or something in support. A glance at the clock told me I was early enough to make a coffee and sit with Pete to keep him company. I suggested as much, and he headed to the break room to make them while I went to my desk to dump my stuff.

Not long after, we sat, both of us laughing when I told him about Aiden's surfing hilarity, not believing

I hadn't mentioned it before over the past couple of weeks.

Pete snorted, saying, "I remember one of the surfing activities last year, and he did something similar then."

"He did?" I asked, amused, more than happy to not only be talking about Aiden but keep the conversation light.

"Oh, yeah!" He placed his empty mug down before continuing. "I don't think he managed to stay on his feet long enough for the bouncing thing, but I swear, his face every single time he wiped out..." He lapsed into a low chuckle. "...hilarious, best thing ever. You know, he's so uptight and all untouchable and shit, yet he knows how to face-plant on a wave with impressive skill."

My smile froze on my mouth at his words. Unease slithered along my skin, not liking one bit that he thought Aiden was any of those things. When I remained quiet, my laughter not following, his eyes widened. "Shit, you know, it's just he kept to himself and has never really got to know any of us really well."

The challenge was on my tongue, wanting to push this, but this was Pete, who was dealing with a nightmare of a situation. It was that thought alone that made me swallow my gut reaction and offer a tight smile. It was all I could manage. "It's all good." The lie rolled off my tongue. I flicked a look at the clock on the wall, seeing it was close to nine thirty. The relief swirling through me had guilt brewing right alongside it. But at least with Pete going to his meeting, I could shake off the unease.

"Damn, yeah, that's the time," Pete said quickly, his gaze having followed my own. "I best get going. Perhaps I can meet you after for a walk, if you're planning on going."

My hesitation was easy to interpret, and from the splash of colour crawling across Pete's cheeks, he read it loud and clear. "Honestly, don't worry, another time, yeah?" he said, not giving me time to answer. And then he was gone, and my guilt renewed.

Sure, I was disgruntled about his offhand comment about Aiden, but it was more to do with the date. I sighed, feeling completely shit about the non-verbal brush-off I'd given him. Standing, I picked up the empty mugs and cleared everything away, figuring I'd catch up with Pete tomorrow. That way, I could apologise and explain that my reaction wasn't really about him.

It had been a shit of a day.

Memories of my sister weighed me down. They were made heavier by my concern for Pete. I was eager for fresh air and a clear head. I sat on the sand, gaze cast out to sea, looking for nothing more than escape. I wouldn't find it.

Aiden had texted me twice and called me once. Each time he went unanswered, but with this second call, I picked up. The last thing I wanted to do was worry the man.

"Hey, Riley, you okay?"

I smiled despite my heavy heart, wondering how he'd known not to give up trying to reach me, and grateful that he seemed to know something was amiss.

"Hey," I answered quietly. "Yeah, just on the beach. Sorry I didn't pick up." I didn't offer him an excuse, not wanting to give him a bullshit reason.

"No worries. Just..." Aiden hesitated. "You sure you're okay?"

I really wasn't. I shrugged, despite knowing he couldn't see me.

"Riley, you there?"

"Yeah," I croaked before slamming my mouth shut, hating I'd given myself away.

"What beach are you at?" Concern flittered through his words, warming me.

"Noosa. About to head home, though."

"Okay," he said slowly. There was a pause before he asked, "What's wrong?"

I winced, swallowing back emotion. After a breath, I blinked rapidly, taking control of myself. "I called for an update on my sister today." Surprise warred with my relief that I'd shared the words.

"Tanya?" he asked, his own surprise pitching his voice. I'd shared stories about my sister, told him about the adventures we got up to as kids, explained how she was my rock growing up with my arsehole parents. Each time it had always been about the past, for obvious reasons. And in the tone he'd pitched her name, I wouldn't be surprised if he'd expected her to no longer be alive—the past tense I used always part of every story I shared.

"Yeah."

"She okay?" His voice was hesitant, concern lacing those two words.

I gave a humourless snort, more at my emotions swirling around me and my disbelief that I was sharing this with him, despite my earlier vows to the contrary.

"Riley, just give me an hour and a half, yeah? I'll meet you at yours."

God, how I wanted that, wanted Aiden to turn up and make it all okay. It just never would be, and I certainly didn't deserve his comfort. "No." My response was quiet and at war with my heart beating out *yes*. "Honestly. I'm just going to head home, eat, and have an early night. It's not been the best of days, but I'll call you in the morning."

"But if I came—"

"It's fine, Aiden. I'm good." The lie I didn't want to say left my mouth, tasting bitter. "I'll call you in the morning."

I waited silently for him to respond and pulled my gaze away from the calm ocean, the peaceful waves too at odds with my spiralling emotions. After a few moments of quiet, he spoke. "Okay, but promise to call me if you need me. You know I'm here for you, yeah?"

I nodded blindly, the tears I refused to shed preventing me from doing anything else. I cleared my throat and croaked, "Thanks. I'll talk to you tomorrow." I ended the call, unable to speak anymore, and slammed my eyes shut.

Shit, each anniversary of the crash was a fucked-up day for sure, but this year, it seemed to hit me harder, and I had no idea why. Sure, I'd be sad and angry and all the emotions in between, but in public and like this.... I usually had a stronger hold on my emotions.

I huffed out a breath and opened my eyes, returning my focus to the tame ocean and the darkening sky. The water was doing nothing to help. Giving in, I stood and headed to my car. My steps faltered when I saw Pete parked next to it. His hands were shoved deep in his pockets, and the smile he sent my way was subdued and a little nervous.

My brows dipped low. "Hey. You looking for me?"

He nodded. "Yeah, sorry. I know you wanted some space... or at least I think that's what you want, but I felt crap about earlier and didn't like the way we left things. Figured you'd be here." He shrugged.

My shoulders sagged, not quite sure how I felt about him tracking me down. Deep in my gut, I knew I didn't want to be alone, quite possibly for the first time in fifteen years. But it was the man I'd just turned down on the phone whose comfort I wanted. I wanted to kick myself for pushing him away.

I gave myself a mental shake, figuring tomorrow I'd talk to Aiden and tell him more about Tanya, explain about my scar, which he'd kissed and traced a time or two. Each time he had, the affection caressed me, but to share with him meant prising open barely healed wounds. Tomorrow I'd make sure I was ready to do just that.

"It's okay," I finally answered Pete, happy I'd done so when his tense shoulders eased a little. "Just one of those days, you know?" I gave a one-shoulder shrug. I finished the short walk to my car. "How'd you get on at work today?" I didn't add that I'd deliberately made myself scarce earlier, not willing to see him and deal with our previous conversation.

"Good, thanks. All sorted, which is a relief."

"I bet. And where's Georgie now?"

"With Mina. She's having a good day, and her neighbour said she'd pop in on her. I promised I'd only be a couple of hours."

I smiled sadly, thinking about his and his sister's whole situation, wondering briefly how he still managed to smile.

"I'm about to head home," I said, then hesitated before offering, "You're free to come over for a coffee before you have to race off."

"Yeah," he said with what I thought was a relieved sigh. The action, the sound immediately reminded me this was a man who was hurting, bad. I got it. I seriously did. Pete heading this way was his only attempt of escapism for a little while, finding normalcy in a life full of shit that was out of his control. And because of that, I threw him a genuine smile.

"You know the way. See you in a few."

It didn't take long to navigate the darkening streets and for me to find my way home. Pete was on my tail. When I pulled up, my thoughts immediately went to Aiden and his concern. I shot off a text.

Me: I didn't mean to worry you. Going to make coffee and food, then head to bed. I'll call you as soon as I'm up.

Grabbing the door handle just as Pete pulled up, I opened my phone again, shooting off another text.

Me: Miss you. X

I smiled in the shadowy interior, feeling more content after reaching out to Aiden. There was no doubt I cared about the man a lot. More than I'd cared about any other guy. I saw a future for us together, actually wanted that pretty desperately. I wasn't there yet, at the love stage, I didn't think, but I missed him when we weren't together. Not only that, but I thought about him constantly. And with almost every thought, and definitely every time I saw him or heard his voice, wings took flight in my stomach, just as my heart flipped over itself.

The whole shebang of feelings exhilarated me. True, my terror for opening up fully, letting him have all of me, kept me grounded, but those wings were perseverant and strong. I wondered how much longer before their power let loose and allowed me to soar.

Chapter Ten

AIDEN

WORRY CHASED ME THE WHOLE DRIVE. SOMETHING was off, and I didn't like it one bit. With everything that had happened with James, fear of falling and hurting again remained close by, just in the shadows of my mind. But Riley wasn't James.

When James's illness had destroyed the life we'd built together, it had left me wrecked, my own version of broken. The last couple of years we'd had together had been challenging, and our relationship had been on the cusp of breaking; it didn't make the hurt easier.

Instead, guilt clasped on to my grief that I'd pushed him to the point of no return.

But Riley was strong, together, and what we had was on the verge of something spectacular. I knew that, yet I pushed the speedo up a few more kilometres as I overtook a truck, just wanting to get to him and see for myself he was okay.

I exhaled when I saw the approaching junction to pull off. Riley didn't live far away from the highway, so in a few short minutes, I'd be able to breathe again. A humourless laugh escaped me, knowing full well I was overreacting, but I cared about Riley, a hell of a lot. Sure, rationally, I didn't expect him to be in any danger, but when he'd mentioned his sister, my internal alarm bells had rung. Hell, from all the times he'd mentioned his sister, which wasn't very often, I'd assumed she died. I winced at the thought, feeling shit for having assumed rather than clarifying. Though, it didn't seem quite right to be blurting out a question like that.

A few minutes later and a few turns, I was pulling into his street.

A few streetlights dotted around, a luxury my place didn't have since I lived in the sticks. I pulled up outside, brows narrowed when I recognised the car on the driveway. Pete was here.

Immediately, my gut churned, a bite of dread snapping at me as I exited my ute. Clamping my jaw together, I exhaled heavily through my nose as I made my way to the door, willing my heartbeat to settle and stop pounding so heavily that I could barely hear the cicadas.

They were friends, I reminded myself. The memory of Riley's texted words lit up in my mind. Coffee, food, bed. At the door, I forced my jaw to relax, inhaled deeply, and stretched out my neck before raising my arm and knocking.

The thirty-second wait seemed to last ten times that while my brain threatened to travel into territories I had no desire to go.

He's not James.

As the thought whispered into my mind, the door opened. I lifted my gaze, and it settled immediately on Riley. His eyes widened, brows jerking high, then my name fell from his lips with a question before a smile spread across his mouth, reaching his gaze.

The reaction was fast, and I chose to believe genuine. Immediately, I stepped up to Riley without a word and wrapped him in my arms, settling a not-too-gentle kiss on his lips.

His grunt sounded surprised, but there was no hesitation as he opened to my needy tongue, no pause as his arms wound around me. I blocked out everything but him. Riley's touch, his taste, his warmth—I wanted it all, wanted him to be mine so fiercely that a sweep of possessiveness thrummed throughout the length of my body.

My hand traced up his spine, landing on the back of his head, holding him to me.

A groan slipped between us, and for a moment, I was unsure whose it was. I soon realised it was Riley, and the knowledge ramped my need higher.

A loud cough cut through my focus that had been 100 percent on Riley. The man in my arms pulled away instantly, but his gaze met mine, and a delicious heat hit his cheeks.

"So that's definitely my cue to get out of here." Pete's voice was amused, laughter evident.

Riley broke our eye contact and turned, and I glanced around him, stepping to his side slightly to see Pete. The guy looked wrecked. Exhaustion laced his features, making me feel guilty as hell there'd been a moment of doubt churning my gut before I'd knocked on the door.

"Pete," I greeted, offering him a chagrined smile. "Good to see you." I cleared my throat. "Uhm, sorry about that."

"Good to see you too, Aiden. And a greeting like that, hell, I don't think you've anything to be sorry for. It's the way every man should greet their boyfriend. But damn—" He fanned himself and smiled. "—make sure you don't have single friends around in the future. Not sure I can handle the heat with my wicked dry spell." He finished off with a laugh, but there was a tightness to his eyes, a slight strain in his voice.

"You don't have to run off," Riley said, his tone gentle, and I figured he was feeling shitty about his reaction to me all but pouncing on him. Renewed guilt clawed at me. Riley had told me how much Pete was struggling, and me being the arsehole I was, hadn't thought too much about it beyond general mutters of sympathy.

I knew better. Should *be* better.

"Honestly, please don't rush off because I'm here. Me being here was unplanned." I forced myself to do the right thing and said, "If you guys were in the middle of something, I can go."

"No." Riley angled to look at me as the one word punched out of him, the power behind it taking me by surprise.

I studied his eyes, seeing sadness flickering in their depths, reminding me exactly why I'd turned up unannounced in the first place. I nodded at him and offered a reassuring smile while placing my hand on his hip, squeezing lightly.

He blinked as if saying a silent thanks and

turned back towards Pete. "Honestly, you don't have to go," he said, but Pete was smiling softly and shaking his head, hand going to his pocket. He tugged out his keys.

"I have to get back anyway to check on things. I'll see you tomorrow at work." Pete glanced at me and gave me a chin lift. "Have a good night."

"Yeah, you too," I offered, stepping out of the doorway and more fully into the hallway to let him leave.

I watched as Riley walked him out of the house. They spoke quietly and patted each other on the back in a half-hug. While I didn't exactly like it, I kept my mouth shut, knowing full well I was being ridiculous.

When Riley stepped back inside and closed the door, he turned to face me, hands moving behind him to lean against the door.

"Hey," I offered, my nerves a little jittery now we were alone. I'd gone against his wishes by rocking up even though he'd told me not to.

"You came," he said, voice gruff and a hint of something else there that I'd never heard before.

"It sounded like you needed someone." I flicked my gaze to the door. Pete had been here; he'd had a friend. "I shouldn't have crashed." I held back my wince.

"Pete hijacked me after my walk." He shrugged, and I bobbed my head in response. Riley remained quiet a beat or two after that and swallowed hard before saying, "Thank you for coming."

I exhaled deeply. "I couldn't not."

At my words, his lips tilted up. "You eaten?" he asked, his tone changing, a glimmer of lightness there.

I nodded. "Yeah."

"Can you stay the night?"

"If you want me to."

"Definitely."

I held my hand out, a silent request for him to take it. He did so, his large, beautiful body heading my way in sure strides as I said, "Let me take care of you."

He clasped my hand. Before I could turn and lead him away, his strong arms wrapped around me. I held him close as he buried his head against my neck and inhaled, squeezing my back lightly as he did so.

I had no idea what was going on with Riley beyond a clue about his sister and the fact he was hurting. "I've got you, baby," I whispered close to his ear, the endearment coming easily. That he hurt didn't sit well in my gut or my heart. While I doubted I could take away whatever ate at him, I would try like hell to make tonight easier for him, and every night he was willing to give me.

We showered together. Beneath the spray of the warm water, I washed Riley down, the first time I'd ever done such a thing. My previous relationship had been passionate and volatile. Things between the two of us were different from anything I'd experience before, and I admitted to myself, a soft whisper in my brain, what we had was so much better than I could ever have hoped for.

I peppered his skin with a trail of light kisses, a sudsy washcloth following the path my mouth had taken. The moment was peaceful, gentle, and just what he needed if his content sighs and relaxing shoulders were anything to go by.

I didn't push my kisses to anything hotter, despite my dick nudging me to do just that. There were different ways to care for someone, and this way, a first for me, was kinda nice.

When I flipped off the water, Riley's eyes sprang open in surprise.

"Shit," he mumbled, "is it possible to sleep standing up?"

I chuckled at his sleepy voice and dotted a soft kiss on his lips. "Come on. Let's get dried off and get to bed."

He nodded, his gaze soft as it connected with my own.

We dried ourselves off and made our way to his room. I tugged back the cool, crisp sheet, and Riley shuffled under the cover, a sweet smile on his mouth. Before making my way to the other side of the king bed, once again I pressed my mouth to his, just the lightest brush and connection. He looked so damn peaceful and sexy like this. But more than that, the frown between his brows had eased over the past thirty minutes. I wanted it to stay that way.

When I clambered under the sheet and sidled up to Riley, his large arms scooped me up, all but hauling me close to his side. I moaned in appreciation, loving the contact and the touch and appreciating the newness of being cocooned.

In my one committed relationship and the few hook-ups I'd had over the years, I'd always been the bigger guy, never really by design. Having strong arms wrapped around me was a whole lot of nice, comforting, and I didn't feel an iota of guilt for luxuriating in that, despite me being here to comfort Riley, not the other way round.

"Thank you," Riley said quietly, angling his head and loosening his grip enough so I could ease back a little and see his face. "I'm happy you came."

Warmth washed over me. I'd made the right decision. "Me too. I wasn't sure if I was overstepping," I admitted.

He shook his head. "You're not. I thought I should be alone." A small shrug followed, but there was nothing casual about it. "Stupid, really. I was playing the martyr card."

Worry vied for dominance in my chest, pushing away the warmth from a moment ago. That deep frown had reappeared between Riley's brows. But from the looks of things, he wanted to talk, and there wasn't a chance I'd be stopping him.

I wanted to carry it all for Riley, share the burden and the pain right alongside him. Doing so would make the happiness, the laughter, the gentleness between the two of us that much sweeter.

I didn't respond to his words. Instead, I gave him an encouraging squeeze around the waist, silently letting him know I was listening and here for him.

"Tanya, my sister, is in full-time care after a car crash we were in."

I paused the stroking of my thumb at his waist a moment before restarting, my mind immediately visualising the large scar on his back and his other hip.

"I'd got into a fight with my folks when home for a visit from uni. They were threatening to not pay the fees of my last year in my degree if I carried on being a 'sicko' and kept screwing up my life by 'choosing' to be gay." His snort was humourless. The sound hit my chest hard and burrowed its way into my chest, hurting for him. "I went out for the night. Got piss drunk, so wasted that I lost my wallet but still had my phone." His voice turned sombre, and he gulped before continuing. "Tanya came and picked me up. If she hadn't have come out to collect me, we wouldn't have been in her crappy little Kia. Wouldn't have been there when the car hit us head-on."

"Shit." The word escaped me on a hiss, and I removed my hand, placing it on his cheek, stroking his lightly whiskered jaw. "What happened?"

"A guy fell asleep at the wheel." He shook his head. "You know how common that is?"

I nodded. I did know. It was scarily high, not surprising considering our huge country and long roads. Hell, I'd driven around some parts of the country and hadn't come across a town for five hours.

"My sister was operated on that night. They had to put her in a coma to help reduce the swelling in her brain. It all pretty much kept going wrong from there."

"I can't even imagine, Riley. Fuck, I'm so sorry you both had to go through that."

Riley's eyes glazed, but he didn't shed a tear. "It was the final nail for my parents. It was my fault. They kicked me out. I managed to get HECS-Help for my last year at uni the following year. I took the year out..." He hesitated, seemed to stumble a little. "It was hard. My sister was my rock. She was a pain in the arse as big sisters are." I smiled a little, and he gave a tentative smile back. "But yeah, that year was hell. On my own, I was dealing with my guilt while trying to work to pay rent in a shitty room. So yeah...."

When he trailed off, I repositioned myself, this time taking him into my arms. I hated he blamed himself. Hated he'd been through so much, and all without the support of his parents. "And what's today?" I asked once he sank into my hold.

"Fifteen years today."

I pressed a kiss to his temple and closed my eyes at the distress in his voice. We remained quiet for a long time, Riley in my arms, me stroking his back and pressing the occasional kiss to his head. My brain was in overdrive, trying to know what to say, how to support him the best way I could.

Our situations were worlds apart, but there was a sameness in loss in many ways. While Riley knew James had died, he still didn't know the circumstances, and now certainly wasn't the time to burden him with that shit.

I continued to hold him, about to ask him when the last time he saw her was, but I held my breath and listened. His breathing had changed. Angling back slightly, I peered at his face. His eyes were shut, and finally, that crease between his brows was gone. I exhaled gently, pleased he was getting some rest.

Today must have been one hell of a battle for him. While a part of me felt a bit irked he hadn't confided in me, I reminded myself it had only been a couple of months we'd been together. Sure, it felt longer, more permanent, but the truth was it had been barely any time at all. It also wasn't like I'd shared with him the truth about James either. But I would, once he was feeling better, and hopefully once he'd opened up to me more about his family.

I swallowed hard at the thought of his reality. I was so damn lucky to have family who loved me, respected me, hell, believed in me. To not have that, which I knew far too many people in the world didn't, was so bloody unfair.

Before I leaned over and switched off the bedside light, I gazed down at the sleeping man beside me. His breaths were soft and even. His one hand was over my waist, his knee between my thighs. Contentment buzzed like a gentle caress at the picture we made together, at just how well we fit.

I liked him a lot. Truth be told, more than liked. I was on my way to the whole heart-flipping kind of love that could quite possibly be the forever kind. There was a possibility of a fantastic future for us, one where I could be his family.

The thought made me shuffle closer and wrap him snugly to me after I pitched the room into darkness.

Chapter Eleven

RILEY

DESPITE THE EMOTIONAL TURMOIL OF SHARING MY past with Aiden, I felt lighter somehow. We hadn't talked it through, he hadn't offered empty platitudes, nor had I gone in depth about the night with him. The thing was, I hadn't needed to. On top of that, his reaction had been what I'd needed, even without me realising it.

We woke early in the morning, much earlier than my alarm was due to go off, but Aiden had to head back to his property to start the day. While I lost a couple of hours of sleep, getting up a sliver before the break of dawn was worth it to be sitting at my small kitchen table drinking coffee with the man who'd helped make my stressful day so much better simply with his presence.

I was grateful as hell for that. For him.

I'd just finished telling Aiden about Pete shifting his hours and then finding me at the beach when I noticed the small frown marring his sun-kissed skin. I paused, my own frown falling into place, asking, "What is it?"

Immediately his brows lifted high, the crease between them disappearing. He gave a small shake of his head and scrunched his mouth up in a way that was the tell-tale sign for both "nothing" and "something is definitely on my mind."

"Huh?" was the response he offered. I didn't buy it.

"Seriously, I was talking about Pete, and you went—" I cut myself off, my eyes widening when I thought about his greeting yesterday. A flutter appeared in my chest, heat spreading in its wake, and my jaw dropped just before I formed a small smile. His greeting yesterday had been hot as hell, totally taking me by surprise, and totally.... I considered the best word, landing on possessive.

"What?" he asked, his gaze zeroing in on me.

I mirrored his scrunched-up mouth from a few moments earlier, adding a shake of my head. There was a twitch of my lips thrown in there for good measure. It was all levels of sweet and surprising. I considered calling him out on it, comparing him to varying shades of green, but with his almost bashful gaze at me, I settled on: "Pete's going through a lot, and I'm glad I'm there for him."

From his expression, it was obvious he knew I was on to him. "Yeah, I know," he answered quickly. "It's good that he has someone."

"Even if I'm that someone?" I asked quietly.

He sighed and laughed lightly. "Am I that obvious?"

My smile was soft as I reached out for him and took his hand. "I expect I'd be reacting the same way as you if the roles were reversed," I admitted, speaking the truth. I'd never before had a real need to feel either jealous or possessive, but I had no doubt I'd be both of those things should the situation call for it.

"Yeah?" he asked, his smile easing and appearing more self-assured.

"Yeah." I nodded. "It's good getting to know Pete better, even though the situation is shitty, but he's absolutely not interested, and I am 100 percent not either. I'm too busy spending time jacking off about this guy I'm seeing when we're not together to have time for anything more." I grinned widely, and he laughed.

"You know, if we saw each other more often, I could help you out with that." Aiden stroked my hand as he spoke, slow, steady strokes that felt so good on my skin.

I considered his words, wishing that was possible. We weren't that far away, but it was still a trek for both of us. Plus, I didn't like the thought of him leaving his pops too often. Us seeing each other mid-week was a rare luxury. We tended to Facetime during the week and spent our weekends together. Usually, I travelled to him where I helped him out with chores in the morning, which was fun and different and less like work for me.

"I'd like to see you more too," I said. "Perhaps on a Wednesday or something, I could speak to the boss about leaving a couple of hours early, making up the time elsewhere so I could come to you straight after work. Maybe even start half an hour later on Thursday."

When his eyes widened a fraction and lit up, his gaze roaming over my face, I squeezed his hand again. This man was so easy to read at times.

"You'd do that?" Hope fuelled his words, filling each syllable with a hint of emotion.

"To get to spend more time with you? Hell yeah, course."

He leaned forwards and cupped the back of my neck, encouraging me towards him. I went so willingly, and our mouths connected. The kiss was gentle, sweet, and I sighed in contentment. He pulled away at the sound, grinning at me.

"Thank you. That would be amazing. Not seeing you in the week is kinda shitty. Pops keeps calling me a moody bastard too," he said with a smile. I chuckled, having no doubt he used other choice words alongside that. "I expect he'll be thanking you a lot."

"You saying I stop you from being a grumpy bastard?"

"Moody," he said, his lips twitching. "I wouldn't dream of being grumpy."

I snorted. "Sure. Not sure your pops would agree with you on that."

Aiden shrugged, his gaze travelling to the clock on my oven. I did the same, figuring he had to get his butt into gear and get going.

"You need to head out."

As he bobbed his head, he huffed out a disgruntled breath. "Looks that way." He stood, picking up our empty mugs and taking them to the dishwasher. When he stacked them rather than leaving them on the side, I smiled inside. I swore to God, this guy was perfect. Possessive kisses and all.

I stood and headed with him to the front door. We paused on the threshold.

"Thanks for yesterday," I said, aware heat had crept into my cheeks. "It meant a lot."

Aiden reached out for me, wrapping his arms around my middle. "I want to be here for you, so anytime, okay?"

"Okay." I nodded. "And I'll see you in a couple of days, right?"

"Damn straight. Just let me know when you're leaving so I know when to expect you."

My heart flipped a little at that. I'd asked Aiden to do the same thing, wanting to know he was safe and what time to expect him, and that Aiden did the same to me... it felt pretty amazing. It had been a long time since anyone had genuinely cared for me, for my well-being. Truth was, it had been my sister, and that seemed all levels of sad to me.

"You okay?" The concern in his voice had me pulling my head out of my butt and focussing on him. I smoothed out my frown, not having realised I'd got so sucked into my thoughts.

A genuine smile curved my mouth despite my melancholy thoughts. "I really am." Truth bled through my words, and when his mouth curved high and he tugged me closer, planting a kiss that had my breath hitching, I knew he heard it too.

He pulled away all too soon, leaving me breathless and my dick twitching, which was pretty much my normal reaction around Aiden.

"Will you think I'm a soft git if I awkwardly ask you something before racing out of here?"

My brows burrowed in confusion. "Uhm... I'm not sure how to answer that."

A blush crept across Aiden's cheeks, pushing my interest to a new level. Before he spoke, he rolled his eyes. "God, I feel like a prick for saying this." The blush reddened to the colour of a sun-ripened tomato. "So, we've never actually discussed our... status." He swallowed, though his gaze held fixed to mine.

My eyes sprung open when my brain processed his words. I couldn't have helped the grin that formed even if I'd wanted to, which I really didn't. A flutter of happiness unfurled and came to life inside me, and seriously, could this guy be any sweeter? Boldness thrummed a steady beat, partly because I had no doubt what Aiden was getting at, but also he was gorgeously awkward with his struggle. I said, "Are you asking me to be your boyfriend?" My cheeks ached in the best of ways from the size of my grin.

Aiden laughed and rubbed his hand over his head, a lopsided smile settling on his mouth. "If you're answer is yes, then that's exactly what I'm asking."

My hand settled on his waist and gave a light squeeze. "That's a big yes from me." I followed up with a press of my mouth to his. I needed to shut up and stop myself from gushing. The words were there, right on the tip of my tongue. Kissing was a much better use of my time and the best way to keep me from embarrassing myself.

Aware of the time and that Aiden needed to leave, I pulled back, a soft smile on my lips.

"Right, so, thanks... yeah... I'm glad that's settled."

I snorted and shook my head. "Me too." I forced myself to step out of his embrace. It would be so easy to press against my boyfriend and get lost in the warmth he offered. I smiled, wondering how long I'd be saying or thinking *my boyfriend* without wanting to high five myself. "Text me when you get home."

"Will do. Have a good day at work."

"You too," I offered. And with a smack to Aiden's arse that had him grunting and me snorting, I waved him off, feeling at peace with this new version of life we were creating together.

"THIS FEELS SUPER AWKWARD," I GROUSED, LOOKING in the mirror once again and trying to flatten my out-of-control hair. It was no use. It was sticking up all over the place, and nothing I did—beyond practically a whole tub of wax—would do the trick.

Aiden chuckled from the sofa, shaking his head at me. "You look gorgeous. Now sit your arse down and stop freaking out."

"You know," I said, turning to him, "ordering me to not freak out doesn't help one bit." I returned my attention back to my reflection, trying to ignore the way my gut filled out my T-shirt just a little too much. Sure, this tee was a few years old now and wasn't quite as snug as it used to be, but the extra weight I carried was noticeable. I scrunched up my nose. It didn't take a genius to work out why this was bothering me now.

For weeks, Aiden had shown nothing but appreciation for my body. Hell, he'd worshipped me in ways I'd never experienced before and never made me feel self-conscious about my body or our physical differences.

But I was about to virtually meet two of his close friends, Mel and Geffen. Knowing Aiden as well as I thought I did, I couldn't imagine his friends being cruel or shallow, but Aiden was a hunk of man. No joke, he was fit and gorgeous. I didn't want his friends taking one look at me and wondering what he was up to.

"Seriously, you look decidedly fuckable," Aiden said, amusement in his words. A quick glance in his direction, and I saw the way his gaze roamed my back, my arse, landing on my face, and all in clear appreciation.

"We could do that now instead if you want. I'll even do that thing that you like with my tongue," I offered, completely not jesting and up for anything but taking this video call.

His eyes seemed to darken, and his tongue slipped out and wet his bottom lip. I grinned while my stomach flipped over at the heat directed my way. And here I thought I was lousy at this seduction thing. It appeared I wasn't half bad.

I turned fully towards Aiden, hand at the button on my canvas shorts. I flicked it open, and his eyes narrowed, first on my hand, then on my face.

"Don't you dare."

My grin grew, and I went for my zip. "What's wrong?" I asked, my voice low, traces of humour evident in my tone. I put my hand in my shorts and gripped my dick, squeezing.

"Fuck, Riley. You trying to kill me?"

He still hadn't made a move. Instead, he stared at me with laser focus, gaze drifting between my cock and my face, eyes flaring. Using my other hand to hold on to the material of my shorts, I made to tug my dick out, only to freeze when his phone rang, the ringer for FaceTime filling the space.

"Fuck," he said again, this time adjusting his cock in his shorts and shooting daggers at me. Somehow I found it in me to laugh as I slipped myself back in, careful to tuck myself away—something I was always super cautious about, considering my past disaster. When I'd told Aiden about the foreskin and zipper incident, he'd supported me with commiserative winces and howls of laughter.

"Come on, baby," Aiden said, holding his hand out to me, his tone holding tenderness that made me gooey. That combined with his use of "baby" was my absolute undoing.

The ringing continued, doing an excellent job at deflating my erection. Giving in, I sat beside Aiden, and he pressed his lips to mine, taking my breath away with the intensity despite the noisy ring and the shortness of the touch. "They'll love you," he said, just before he turned his attention to his phone and hit Accept.

Two men appeared on the screen. I tried to take in as much about them as possible and was sure they were doing the same thing.

The one guy was petite. I imagined a good head shorter than his husband when standing. His eyes were wide, a piercing blue, and kind. Perhaps it was his giant grin directed through the screen that made them seem that way.

"I was beginning to think you were too busy getting"—he waggled his blond eyebrows—"*busy* to answer the call. Just don't drop the camera. I don't want to see your junk," he said, chuckling. "Hey, Riley, I'm Mel. How's it going?"

My shoulders relaxed at his friendly tone and playful greeting. "Yeah, good, thanks, Mel. Good to meetcha."

My attention turned to the man at his side, Geffen. He was broad-shouldered, thickset. While his size didn't take me by surprise necessarily, he was simply so very different from his husband. The contrast was striking, with the only thing similar being the broad, seemingly genuine smile on his face.

His teeth gleamed against the darkness of his skin, legit making me envious as hell that they were so white and perfect. Dark, almost black eyes peered back at me, the skin around them scrunching a little as he grinned. "Hey, Aiden, Riley, good to see you both. 'Bout time you crawled outta the love nest or whatever you have going on there to finally make a call," he said pointedly to Aiden, who smirked and rolled his eyes.

"Love nest?" He snorted. "No idea what you guys are into, making forts or some shit. But yeah, life's been busy."

I glanced at Aiden, who gave me his eyes and followed through with a wink. His hand moved to my thigh, and he squeezed lightly.

"I can see that," Mel said, his smile still in place. "Pleased you came up for air though. So, Riley, Aiden said you work in IT or something?"

"Yeah," I said. "Programming and data management. Pretty boring stuff," I added, completely underselling what I did, used to people glazing over when I started talking about work.

"It's all lies," Aiden cut in before Mel could respond, taking me by surprise. "He works for a medical research company, doing important, complicated shit that I'm clueless about, but what he's doing and has done is important."

Warmth spread in my chest, a gentle caress of acceptance and pride that he'd talk about me this way. I coughed a little awkwardly, despite the glow buzzing in my chest. "Not sure about that."

Aiden quirked his brow at me, face completely angled my way. "You're brilliant. Don't knock it." My gaze searched his, and all I could do was nod and smile, the warmth expanding and settling soul deep. When he turned his attention back to his phone, he moved his hand from my thigh and took my hand in his. The light thumb stroke against my skin made it hard to think and keep my head straight.

I looked back at the screen to see both men's eyes volleying between us. Mel was biting his bottom lip while Geffen's eyes were soft, and his grin had turned into a gentle smile.

I fought hard not to shift uncomfortably under their scrutiny, but at least they seemed to think Aiden's behaviour was sweet or something, which it totally was.

"Okay," Mel said, coming out of whatever stupor he was in, "we're inviting ourselves to yours for Australia Day next year, just so you know."

Aiden laughed. "Really? That's great. I'll be sure to air out the swags."

Geffen's wide-eyed horror made me laugh. "Hell no," he said quickly, his voice higher than a few moments ago. "You put me anywhere near a swag or even a tent, and you'll find yourself stranded at that farm of yours."

My brows dipped as I laughed, wondering what he meant.

Mel rolled his eyes at his husband. "Geffen's a mechanic. It wouldn't be the first time he's dismantled an engine because someone's pissed him off."

I laughed louder. "Seriously?"

Mel nodded as Geffen said, "Some things, like sweaty canvas, are no joke."

"Right," Aiden sassed, "and it's nothing to do with that time you found yourself setting up your swag on an ant nest and were bitten a few times."

"The fuck? A few times, my arse. Those bastard things were everywhere. I nearly went into anaphylactic shock or some shit."

Aiden chuckled loud and hard while Mel shook his head, smirking.

"You had what, maybe five bites, and the 'shock' was you running around like you'd just encountered a swarm of killer bees or something."

Geffen narrowed his eyes at Aiden, his lips twitching ever so slightly. He then turned his attention to me. "Don't listen to a word this arsehole says. It's all lies. Either he's underexaggerating to make himself feel better or overexaggerating to make himself look good. Has he told you about his shark attack yet when he went on a trip near the Barrier Reef?"

The reactions from all three happened simultaneously, though all very differently. Geffen sat with a shit-eating grin on his face, flipping Aiden off, Mel laughed loudly to the point of tears, and Aiden shouted, "The fuck. Seriously, man, you had to go there."

Wide-eyed, I glanced at all of them in succession. "Okay, this I've got to know. Shark attack?" My brows dipped in question when I looked at Aiden.

"I barely survived." His voice was monotone, though the twinkle in his eyes was filled with laughter. "It's something I can't talk about without the horror of the day hitting me full force. I know you love me too much for that." Immediately, Aiden's eyes widened, his mouth dropping open before he slammed it shut. I saw some movement on the screen and quite possibly heard a gasp. Me? I froze, sure the words were just a simple phrase, something

I'd said a time or two to friends in the past even. But when it came to Aiden and me and what we shared, the words didn't seem as flippant.

"With a lead-up like that," I said as soon as my brain caught up, wanting to break through the sliver of tension, "there's no way you're getting out of telling me." I grinned at him, aware he searched my face. Not sure exactly what he was looking for, I squeezed his hand, trying to reassure him that I was here, and honestly, I wasn't sure what else I was aiming for. All I knew was anything even related to my feelings for Aiden would not be dissected now, while we had an audience who neither Aiden and I had paid attention to for a good thirty seconds or so, but which felt more like minutes.

"Mel," I deflected, ignoring how his bright blue eyes seemed to be drinking in everything unfolding before him. "Who needs to be telling the story?"

"Definitely me," Geffen said quickly, the speed of it making me chuckle and Aiden groan.

"Fine, have at it." Aiden then mouthed, "Swag," at Geffen, and I grinned at this sillier side to him. It was fun and carefree. While I'd seen him be both before, never with the same level of banter. It was good to see.

Chapter Twelve

AIDEN

I was running late, so I agreed to meet Riley at the beach. Today we were paddleboarding. It wasn't something I'd actually done before, and while I wasn't super keen, it had to be better than surfing, plus I got to have some fun with Riley. It was the latter that had me excited to be pulling up in the car park.

He was already here, standing with Trey, Mark, and Pete. That Pete was here surprised me, as I was sure Riley said he couldn't make it. Shoving that thought aside, I exited the car, my gaze still in the direction of the group of men.

Riley's gaze immediately found mine, and that smile that I swore lit up my whole day appeared on his handsome face. He said something to the small group and strode over to me, his long legs eating up the concrete.

I smiled at his eagerness, always feeling that slight flutter of relief that he was as happy as me to see each other.

"Hey," he greeted and stepped up close, his lips on mine, albeit too briefly. But then he followed up with his nose in the crook of my neck, inhaled, and pressed a tender kiss there.

Every single time he did this, my dick jerked and my heart just about exploded with how full it felt.

"Hey, yourself. You doing okay?"

Riley nodded. "Even better now."

I couldn't agree more. Life had been a combination of perfect with the same old routine of work and life. But it was the latter—the weekends and those Wednesday nights—that had shifted the "life" part to perfect.

For the past three weeks, we'd managed to make that extra day a week work, and I had no idea how I'd coped before it.

"Good. Were you hanging around for me?"

"Yeah, but it's all good. No one minded."

I bobbed my head in relief. When I'd woken this morning, it was to a couple of broken wires in the fence around the Rosebud paddock. It had thrown me off schedule to get my basic chores done before heading to the Sunny Coast for the Outback Boys meetup. But I was here now, and with Riley looking eager and clearly happy to see me, it was easy to push away my bad mood when I'd been sorting repairs at six this morning.

"You need to change?" he asked, eyeing my jeans.

"I just need to grab my rashie. I've got my boardies on."

"Is it in the boot?" he asked, stepping around to the back of my car.

"Yeah, thanks." I followed him, then paused, undoing my button and zipper. My eyes were glued to him, though, loving his reaction when I did such things.

His groan preceded his stink eye. "You know I'll only get you back."

I chuckled low. "Is that right?"

"You know you look ridiculously sexy when you undress that way." His right brow quirked high as he spoke.

"I don't know any other way of taking off my jeans." I didn't keep my grin at bay as I spoke, loving that something so simple riled him up.

"Uh-huh. You keep believing that, wisearse." He tossed my rash vest at me. It landed on my head, and

I laughed loudly as I pulled it away and then stepped out of my jeans. "You need the sun lotion?"

"Yeah, please."

It didn't take long for us to be lathered up in lotion and heading over to the rest of the group. After quickly apologising and thanking them for waiting for me, the instructor made quick work of walking us through paddleboarding logistics.

It seemed pretty straightforward, but so much relied on balance and coordination. Plus, I wasn't the lightest guy ever. I expected that wouldn't play in my favour.

We headed to the shoreline with gently lapping waves, having come to a more sheltered spot, which was great for this, I supposed, but awful for something like surfing.

"How long do you reckon before I sink or capsize this board?" I asked. The five of us had headed a few metres away, all of us naturally splitting into smaller groups. It was something new for me. Usually I just hung out with Frank or off to the side, unless people needed help with something. But that was before Riley. Because of his friendship with Pete, it led me to be in the group with Mark and Trey.

It was surprisingly easy. While I'd distanced myself from getting too close to anyone when I'd moved east and then joined Outback Boys, I was aware half-arsed gossip around the whys of that had filtered through the group. But despite me being standoffish, Mark and Trey hadn't even done a double-take with me being practically a limpet on Riley's side.

In the last few meetups, they'd accepted Riley and I were together and that apparently, I was more sociable. And I was glad for it. I'd already known they were good guys, and now I could count on them in my small group of friends too.

"Based on you and your surfing skills, I'd say five seconds," Mark said with a kind chuckle and finished off with a smile.

"Ha! I'm impressed you think I can make it that long."

We stopped and placed our boards and equipment down, me eyeing the long white board with reservation. Give me a rope and a rockface any day of the week over this. Water with waves was so not my thing. I imagined it was to do with me spending most of my life in the middle of red sand, with the closest beach being about fifteen hundred kilometres away up in Darwin.

"I'll put five on thirty seconds."

I whipped my gaze to Riley, who was grinning

widely at me.

"What?" he asked, not looking at all sorry for upping the ante and making my inability to balance on water a bet. "Thirty seconds means I have faith in you."

I quirked my brow at him as laughter from the guys surrounded us.

"I'm in for ten seconds," Pete added, his own smirk plastered on his face.

When Mark opted for twenty, and Trey for fifteen, I shook my head at them all. "Bloody bastards, the lot of you," I complained to them, my own grin not going anywhere. "In that case, I'm going for thirty-five. A nice twenty-five bucks will buy me some decent grub after this, and all thanks to you non-believers."

"That's the fighting spirit," Pete sassed.

"Uh-huh, you just keep telling yourself we're buying you grub," Riley said with a chuckle.

I stood with the paddle and shot a look at the man who made my heart flip over itself. "You're supposed to be on my side."

He stepped towards me and planted a kiss on my lips. We both ignored the catcalls, and when he pulled away, I was a little dizzy from the heat that had immediately unfurled inside me.

"I'm on your side, Aiden." He stepped back, saying, "But I also don't want to pay for my steak."

I kicked water at him and shook my head, chuckling.

"Come on already. Get your arse into the water," Pete said. I flicked a glance at him as he looked around at us. "Trey, you've got your watch. You're in charge of timing."

"On it," Trey responded, looking both eager and amused.

"I swear you guys need to get out more."

"Hey," Trey said. "This is getting out more, and seeing you fall on your arse with such grace is a pastime we all enjoy."

Mark chuckled at his side. "It's only because we think you're awesome." A shit-eating grin followed.

"Sure it is." I rolled my eyes, grabbed the board, and dragged it out into the ocean, amusement and lightness dancing in my chest with each step. It was this camaraderie I hadn't had in forever. Being with James had been incredible at first, until it hadn't. His mental health had made things beyond stressful. At times he was violent, nudging into abusive. Some of my old friends hadn't understood why I'd stuck around, but I'd loved the man when he was well and even when he wasn't doing so great. But more than that, he tried to get help, tried to function with the meds he was prescribed. It was in the difficult times —those when he was low when he refused any support—that my resentfulness had grown, but I'd tried my hardest to keep it at bay, knowing it was his illness I hated rather than James.

And over time, particularly the last year of his life, my friends had drifted away, not willing to stick around to witness my hurt or the drama. It had been shit, but it was their prerogative, and I supposed it let me know exactly who I could count on.

"Thirty seconds!" Riley hollered out to me, humour evident in his tone. "You've got this, baby."

I shot him the stink eye, which he immediately laughed at. The arsehole knew how the single endearment got me hot under the collar.

"Hey, no sweet-talking and trying to get him to throw the comp for you," Pete said with a laugh.

I snorted, knowing full well it was going to be Pete who won.

Five seconds, here I come.

I waded out until I was about knee-deep in the gently lapping water. Once there, I angled to the side and glanced at the guys still on the sand. My gaze flicked to Riley. His smile was wide, and the wink he shot me made me grin back and shake my head. I held the board by the edges and pushed up, lying flat, much like I would a surfboard. Once balanced, I worked my way to my knees, gripping a little tighter as the board wobbled and bobbed with the small waves.

When the catcalls and cheers started up, I laughed, looking back at the small group. That they were taking the piss in their own supportive way made it easier to breathe and simply have fun with the moment.

"Yeah, yeah," I called back. "Just get ready with that timer."

"All over it." Trey gave me a thumbs up.

With my hands on the sides of the board, my attempt at stabilising the damn thing, according to the instructor, I moved one foot at a time until they were flat and found purchase. The motion was slow and steady and entirely unlike surfing at this point.

Knees bent, I leant back, my chest now vertical, before straightening my legs and standing. I wobbled precariously, the movement making me extend my arms, my right hand gripping the paddle. A fresh roll of light laughter from the shore came with my unsteady footing, alongside Trey's shout of "Now!"

Shifting my foot, a bare inch at a time, to try to

stop simply falling and slamming into the water, I moved them till they were inline and parted.

"Seven seconds!"

"Shit!" Pete shouted, laughter in his voice.

I grinned, feeling a little more comfortable. Hell, maybe I had this after all.

Bending my knees slightly, I straightened my back, needing to find my equilibrium.

"Twelve seconds."

I needed to lift my head so I wasn't simply staring at my feet. The instructor had said something about using my hips to shift my weight. Aware that the board teetered a little—not quite a wobble, but it certainly wasn't steady—I figured I had to shift my weight to my left a fraction.

"Sixteen seconds!" Trey shouted, and new cheers went up.

I grinned wider and, this time, dared to look up, loving the shit-eating grin Riley directed my way.

Okay, so I needed to use my hips to shift my weight, not my feet.

I thrust my hips like a goddam porn star, immediately realising that was absolutely the wrong thing to do. I jerked forwards and attempted to correct myself. I failed with a "Fuck!" as I toppled to my left, legs sweeping up and high, and my arse hitting the water before I submerged.

I broke the surface, wiping my face of saltwater and laughing. Loud cheers and hollers greeted me, and the guys were clapping, going completely over the top with the celebration.

Mark's cheer was extra exaggerated as he shouted, "Pay up. Totally called it!" The rest of our small group groaned, his husband shoving him a little in the shoulder.

Then, almost as one, they picked up their boards and paddles and headed out in my direction, all smirking and chatting animatedly.

Riley was before me in a few seconds. "Twenty-two seconds."

"You proud of me?" I asked, my arm wrapping around him. He stepped closer with a large smile and soft eyes.

"Hell yes. Always." He followed up with a hard, quick kiss, and pulled away despite my grumble. "Right, my turn. Thank Christ you guys didn't bet on me, else Pete would have definitely won."

My mouth curved into a gentle smile. "I honestly expected Pete to be winning the bet on me for sure. And you kicked surfing's butt, so I'm sure you've got this."

The look he shot my way had fresh warmth racing a familiar path across my skin. When he looked at me like this, as though I'd said something that he liked, a lot, it was impossible not to look ahead to our future and want everything he was willing to give me.

I wanted all of his smiles, his soft, heated looks, and if he was willing, his heart too. I felt the connection deeply and would do everything in my power to ensure we stayed the course.

"Thanks, baby," he mumbled, his words just for me.

Around us, splashes, laughter, and a few cheers filled the air. Before long, all of us were sort of stable on our boards and attempting to paddle, and with some decent success.

After an hour and just a few moments of falling —this time with no kangaroo-on-acid bounces— Riley and I dragged in our boards and sat on the beach, the gentle waves rolling in and covering our feet and legs.

"You having a good time?" I side-eyed him. His arm pressed against my own as he looked out across the horizon.

"Yeah, definitely. It's actually quite relaxing."

I nodded, agreeing completely. It was nice to do

an activity together where we could still shoot the shit, rather than something more isolating like abseiling or surfing. I turned my thoughts to my call with my sister last night. "I spoke to Emily last night." I leaned back, propping myself up on my hands. Riley peered over at me as I continued. "She's invited us up, and Pops, for a barbie next weekend if you're up for it. It's Timmy's birthday on Friday, so he's having play dates or something with his friends, but she wants a family thing on Saturday afternoon."

I couldn't believe my nephew was going to be six already. The months were racing on by far too quickly. I usually saw him in some shape or form around his birthday, but Emily had sprung the barbie on me last night, demanding Riley come too. I smiled at the thought, knowing she was peeved that she still hadn't met the man who wrapped me up in knots.

"Yeah, sure, I'd love to," Riley responded, offering me a shy smile.

It wasn't a hardship by any means for him to be meeting my sister. Far from it. I wanted him to get to know all the important people in my life. Once Riley had met Emily, that meant there was just Lee, my friend from childhood. And that would happen at some point.

Lee was off travelling overseas for work, so I never knew when to expect him back in the country. At times we'd go a good four months without texting or chatting, and that was okay too. It was just the way it was.

"Great. It'll get my sister off my case," I said with a low chuckle.

"About what? Me?" He leaned back on his hands, mirroring my position, gaze intently on mine.

I snorted. "You could say that. She's pretty keen to meet you." A light pink flushed his skin at my words. I scooted my fingers over behind me on the sand to touch his.

"Should I be nervous about that?" he asked, the smile on his lips conflicting a little with the worry in his eyes.

"Hell no," I answered immediately. "She's gonna love ya." I swallowed hard at the thought, so close to being at that point myself, or at least telling him that. I'd tried to bullshit myself a few times about not quite being there yet. But what the hell did that even mean anyway?

It was too easy to try to compare the love I'd had with James to how I felt about Riley. The emotions that bubbled to the surface every time we were together, and every moment my thoughts turned to him were incomparable. Each time there was a flicker of a spark, which ignited into flames of feelings so bright that it was easy to break through the previous darkness I'd found myself in.

Riley's "Yeah?" drew my attention back to his piercing gaze.

"Yeah. Definitely." I angled towards him, my intention clear. I stroked my thumb up his wrist, only to pause. "Shit, your bracelet." I glanced down at the same time Riley snatched his hand away, cradling his wrist. Something I'd never seen before came to life in his eyes.

His distress was immediate and palpable. He jumped up and searched the ground.

"Hey," I said, jumping up beside him, reaching out for him, but he stepped out of my grasp, his eyes briefly on me before continuing to search. "We'll look on the beach together, okay?" I offered, not quite sure exactly what the significance of the leather bracelets was. My gaze dropped to his other wrist. That bracelet remained in place.

While I didn't think we'd have much luck finding it, I made the effort anyway, uneasy with his reaction. It was likely it had snapped off in the water, and if that was the case, it would be lost.

After fifteen minutes of searching, I returned to

Riley's side. Troubled, I was hesitant to reach out to him. When he turned to me, he seemed less manic and sadder. Unable to resist, I reached out and gripped his bicep. "I'm sorry we couldn't find it," I said quietly.

His sorrowful smile didn't reach his eyes, but he bobbed his head, still circling his bare wrist with his other hand. "It's okay. Thanks for looking with me."

"Of course. I can perhaps get you something new to replace it."

Emotion filled his eyes, taking me by surprise. "Shit, sorry." He huffed out a breath and looked to the sky a moment while I stroked my thumb over his skin. "It's silly." His gaze returned to mine, emotion still present, but he seemed less on edge. "It's just Tanya bought them for me for my birthday that year."

Heartache punched me hard in the gut, and I stepped into his space, forcing him to release his wrist and wrapping him up in my arms. "I'm so sorry, baby. I get it, and it's not silly."

When he hugged me back and exhaled heavily, tension eased from my shoulders. I could totally understand his reaction, but I couldn't help but wonder why he wore them all the time, especially in the ocean in activities like this, if they were so precious. There was no way I'd be a dick and ask him that, though. I assumed he had his reasons.

"You want to get out of here?"

He nodded against my shoulder.

"Come on then. Let's grab the equipment and head back to the car."

We collected everything and waved at Pete, who'd called Riley's name. Even from a distance, I could see the concern on his face. But he had nothing to worry about. Riley was mine, and I'd do everything in my power to make sure he was safe and happy.

After dropping off the boards, jackets, and paddles, we headed towards the vehicles. With each step we took, I wished I hadn't been late so we could be travelling to my place together.

I opened my truck door as Riley opened his car boot to grab our dry gear. Pulling my rash vest off, I dried myself down and glanced at him as he lifted his own rashie to tug over his head.

A blob of black on his wrist caught my attention as he did so, and I narrowed my eyes, wondering what it was. I angled closer. Surprise sparked and came to life when I realised it was ink, a tattoo.

"You have a tattoo?" I asked in surprise, interest having me reach out to take his wrist.

I was aware of his distressed gasp as I held on to his wrist and turned it to look, but my focus zeroed in on what I was seeing.

A semicolon approximately one inch long was imprinted on his wrist.

My eyes widened, my heart picking up speed and pounding loudly in my ears. "The fuck?" My words escaped as a quiet whisper, heavy on my breath and hurting as the syllables released.

"Don't," he said and flinched. But I didn't, couldn't as my gaze moved to the collection of small white lines adjacent to the tattoo.

Scars. Healed cuts.

I released his arm as though his skin burned me and closed my eyes.

Riley had once hurt himself. Perhaps tried to take his life.

The knowledge punched me in the solar plexus, threatening to buckle my knees.

No. Not again.

There was no way I could go through this a second time. Not after James. Not after it had taken me so long to heal, to break through the surface and breathe again.

Riley's tentative "Aiden" had me springing my eyes open. They snagged his immediately. Doubt, hurt, and pain I recognised all too well swirled in their depths.

My head was shaking before I even realised I was making the action. "I can't do this." I backed away, eyes wide, heart breaking even as I saw the devastation crashing into Riley. "I'm sorry, I just can't."

Riley's brows furrowed as he slammed the boot shut, and a new emotion crossed his face. Anger lit him up. "Are you serious?" His voice dropped so low perhaps it would have taken me by surprise if I wasn't caught up in the horror of my memories.

Of finding James.

Finding his limp body, heart still, lungs unmoving.

I shook my head and swallowed hard, wanting to pull my gaze away from the man who made me so incredibly happy and feel at peace.

Riley's jaw tightened, eyes hard despite the moisture swirling in them. "If you want to go, just go." He shook his head once and looked away before his hurt, angry gaze flitted over mine. He looked like he had more to say, but instead, he moved to his door, got in, started the engine, and pulled away. I watched him go, seeing Pete flag him down as I got into my car.

Sadness pulled at me. Threatened to take a firm

grip and drag me so far beneath the depths of despair, I'd never escape. It wasn't what I wanted. I hated it. Hated my reaction, the loss, the self-loathing, the anger. I scoffed. Anger? I was fucking furious.

How could he have done this to me?

I punched my steering wheel in despair, no longer thinking about Riley. James. How could James have made the decisions that led us... *me* to this point of reacting, being so damn terrified of even taking a moment to listen and pause?

I wanted to hate him.

Perhaps I did.

But what was the point?

He was gone.

He'd also not been in control, his illness taking a firm hold of him and refusing to let him go.

James had broken, disappeared. His illness destroyed everything, pushed him to swallow the pills along with a litre of whiskey.

Truth was things hadn't been right in a while. I'd already lost James but had been too terrified, too damn weak to step away and leave. Yeah, love had played a hand, but it was the mess, it was the thought of giving up that had stopped me from doing the right thing for the two of us.

Stubbornness had helped to get me where I was today. Perseverance was a strength, right? Unless it forced you to stay in a challenging relationship with a man who, in the end, refused to accept any support, destroying himself in the process, and tugging you down with him.

And that was the crux of it.

As much as James had crushed me, he'd set me free.

So why the hell was I still contemplating the what-ifs? Why was I allowing Riley, this incredible man, to walk away, letting him believe I didn't want him?

Fuck. My reaction, my horror, my fear.... I had no idea how he would have interpreted my response other than me completely destroying everything we'd built.

Nausea swirled in my gut, making me light-headed. Oh God, the hurt on his face at what I'd said to him, how I'd looked at him.... I shook my head.

It was unforgiveable. What I'd done was beyond excusable.

Fuck.

"Wait." I wrenched open my door and jumped out onto the concrete, searching the area, hoping it wasn't too late. My eyes zeroed in on movement, ears picking up the sound of a diesel engine that had seen better days.

It was too late.

Riley pulled out of the lot. His brakes kicked in briefly, and hope flared to life in my chest. It was extinguished a moment later when the red lights disappeared and the car with the man I shouldn't have let get away vanished with them.

"Fuck."

I hesitated, debating for far too long about whether I should follow him or give him space.

Fists clenched, I looked around for something to hit, to throw. I took a step in the direction of my ute, but I paused when I heard a door opening and closing. A quick glance in that direction, and my gaze fell on a woman with a small child.

My eyes widened at what I'd been about to do. Unclenching my hand, I exhaled before sucking in another breath.

This wasn't James's fault. Not really. Just like he'd made choices, I'd made my own.

Only I was to blame for Riley racing away like I'd torn his tender heart out of his chest.

Chapter Thirteen

RILEY

Sometimes I thought I might break. It wasn't so hard to believe. With all the devastation that had happened over the years, there were times breathing was difficult. But then I'd remember to try, to fight. A brief inhale followed by an exhale.

I wanted to be flippant. Shrug it off and mumble "so the fuck what." But it mattered. Though one thing I was certain of, there was no way on earth I'd break.

I hurt. Yes.

I wanted to lick my wounds and my pride. Sure.

But my heart would remain intact and just keep on beating.

Even as I tried to convince myself of all these things, tried to protect myself from sinking into confusion and despair, emotion clogged in my throat. I swallowed it down, my breath catching and eyes watering with the movement.

I huffed out a breath, refusing to let any tears spill.

I didn't dare look out of the rear-view mirror. Unsure what I'd find, I narrowed my eyes and kept them firm on the road before me. The last place I wanted to go was home. At the intersection, I put my indicator on and went right. Pete would let me wallow for maybe ten minutes before shaking me silly and plying me with cake, since booze was out of the question. Perhaps not the healthiest of ways of dealing with my emotions, but for the moment, it would have to do.

Pete sat at my side, silent and resolute in his quiet support. He had no idea what had me driving away from the beach like someone had lit a fire beneath me, but apparently, my expression had been enough for him to simply open the passenger door and slide inside, wet clothes and all.

"We okay to go to yours?" I asked quietly.

"Of course." I expected him to say more, but he remained quiet.

My shoulders eased when he left me to stew in my own thoughts. Livid didn't even begin to scratch the surface of my emotions. That was too simplistic. Mortification had slammed into me when Aiden had seen my tattoo and then my scars. I couldn't help but be pissed off that *that* had been my immediate reaction.

It had taken me years to shake away my shame, but the look on his face, how he'd staggered away so quickly as though I was contagious or something.... Shame had wrapped around me like a heavy shroud, threatening to buckle my knees.

I shook my head at my thoughts and emotions, the sound of Pete's quiet breathing the only noise in the car.

Aiden could go and screw himself.

After all that had happened with Tanya, on top of my parents cutting me off, I'd spiralled. That first year, I still struggled to remember it all or really understand how I survived.

Vulnerable and filled with guilt, after Tanya's fifth surgery—that one nearly taking her life—I reached the point of despair. A razor, a bottle of cheap vodka, and alone in the shithole room I'd rented, there'd been a sweet release at the first sharp cut, even sweeter with the second, but the fifth, that one much deeper from what the hospital psychologist told me, would have taken my life.

It had been some strange twist of fate that had prevented that from happening. Another tenant had barged into my room by mistake, called an ambulance, and got me to the hospital in time to repair the damage and start my long recovery to getting the help that I needed.

After that, I'd returned to uni to complete my course, kept my head down, and then finally moved east to Queensland. But it was only ten years ago that I got the tattoo.

At that point, I'd survived for five years by myself. I succeeded in getting my degree and got a decent job that paid enough for me to buy a small house. While my mortgage was hefty, the place was still mine. It had been in a random staff training meeting, one of those annoying ones where a specialist came in—this one was about mental health and teamwork and things—where something the guy had said stuck with me.

Courage doesn't always roar. Sometimes courage is the quiet voice at the end of the day saying "I will try again tomorrow."

When I'd got home that day, I'd researched the quote. It was by an American author, Mary Anne Radmacher, who I'd never heard of before. But it had stuck with me, the words weaving around my soul. I was more than aware I'd tried to take my life. There was no denying, no backtracking, it merely was. And ten years ago, in a crappy compulsory training session, I finally understood I had nothing to be ashamed of and that I was courageous and could continue to be so.

That weekend the ink had been the physical reminder that I could take on the world and pick myself up, no matter how hard I sometimes fell.

I trailed my finger over my tattoo without real thought, aware Pete was glancing in my direction. But I didn't stop, didn't cover it up, because fuck that.

I had nothing to be ashamed of, and Aiden, despite how my heart ached and hurt with every beat when I thought of his reaction, would not be my undoing.

It didn't take much longer before we pulled up outside Pete's place. As soon as I parked, I winced, saying, "Your car's still at the beach. I'm sorry."

"Don't sweat it," he said. "You can take me to collect it a little later."

"Yeah, of course." I bobbed my head and glanced out the window at his small weatherboard home.

Pete tentatively touched my arm. "Come on. Let's go grab a coffee."

I nodded and exited the car, following him to his

front door. "Shit, let me go and grab my towel and dry clothes," I said quickly, jogging to my car to get it. When I opened my boot, my gaze landed on my phone. I'd tucked it in there before heading out paddleboarding. I swallowed hard. Already that seemed like so long ago, rather than a few short hours of us teasing Aiden and taking bets on him.

I woke it up, seeing several missed calls, notices about a voicemail, and a couple of text messages too. All from Aiden. I closed it immediately, my heart pounding so hard the sound filled my ears. I couldn't deal with him or anything he had to say right now, if ever.

After placing my phone back down, I scooped up my towel and clothes and made my way back to Pete's. When I pushed the door closed, he called out to me, "Head to the bathroom to dry off. I'm just in my room."

Without a word, I did so, drying myself off and dressing. The entire time, I avoided the mirror, not willing to see just how haunted my eyes would be or how devastated my expression was.

Bypassing my reflection, I wrapped my wet swimmers in my towel and headed to the kitchen. Pete glanced up from preparing coffee when I entered, offering me a tentative smile.

"Just throw those on the draining board." He indicated towards my damp towel.

My smile was automatic, but I didn't feel any lightness as I did so. After I placed my things down, Pete gave a head lift towards the back door.

"Come on. Let's take these outside."

I nodded, aware of how quiet I was being but unable to do much else as I followed him out and sat on the comfy setting he had out there. He placed my steaming mug on a small table, and I positioned myself next to it, exhaling as I did so.

Opposite me, Pete eyed me as he placed his own drink down and sat. "Mina's not expecting me back anytime soon," he said, and he tugged out his phone. "Her neighbour will give me a call if there are any issues."

I bobbed my head and exhaled a little unsteadily. "How are things with Mina?" I asked, latching on to the out of talking about something else.

A tentative smile lifted his lips, making him appear tired and older than his years. "Good days and bad days. But she's making the most of every one."

"And Georgie? She doing okay?"

Pete's eyes lightened a little at the mention of his

niece. "She's amazing, fallen into her new routine with me around so easily."

"That's great."

He bobbed his head and pursed his lips, and immediately I sighed, knowing he was done with distracting me.

"It's all fucked."

His brows shot high at my words. "How so?"

Once again, my thumb went to the tattoo on my wrist. Pete's eyes dropped at the movement, homing in on it.

"Is that a semicolon?" There was no hardness in his voice, no distaste, no accusation.

"Yeah." I pressed my lips together, waiting to see how he'd respond.

He nodded, his gaze roaming my face a moment before he said, "I'm pleased you're here."

Emotion slammed into me thick and fast. Why the hell couldn't have that been Aiden's response? Why hadn't he offered that quiet support and understanding? I clamped my mouth shut, terrified a sob would escape.

Pete's knee jerked, and he seemed to hesitate about how to respond. I just hoped he didn't try to comfort me. I couldn't handle that without breaking down altogether. And while he'd stepped up and our friendship had grown over the past few weeks, he didn't have the comforting arms that I wanted.

"Let me get you water." He stood and squeezed my shoulder lightly as he walked by. Gratitude rolled around me, calming some of the emotion that hovered in my throat. Pete leaving me for a moment helped me get myself under control, so when he returned, I took the glass of water gratefully and felt calm enough to talk.

"Thanks," I said when I'd drained the glass. From the look of it, I figured Pete knew I wasn't only referring to the drink.

He offered me a soft smile. "Do you want to talk about Aiden?"

"Not really."

"Fair enough." His eyes returned to my wrist. "How about that? Do you want to talk about that?"

I considered it before shaking my head. "Not right now, but I will another time." After already going over everything in my head, I didn't have the energy to verbalise all that had happened.

"Just know I'm here, though, okay?"

I smiled. "I know. Thanks."

We continued talking about nothing of signifi-cance for the next hour, giving my nerves time to calm and my head to think straight. By the time I dropped him off at his car, the parking lot empty of the vehicles from our group, I headed home with a promise to touch base with Pete tomorrow. The whole journey back, my heart felt battered, so much so, I wasn't sure it would ever be the same again.

Chapter Fourteen

AIDEN

AFTER I THANKED JERRY FOR FILLING IN FOR ME FOR the few chores I'd intended on doing this afternoon with Riley, I pressed my head back against the headrest before ending the call. There was no way I could head home until I saw Riley. While I had no idea if he'd want to see me, let alone talk to me, I had to try.

Parked outside his house, I glanced down the street, hoping like hell he came home.

I'd screwed up something major. While that was possibly the understatement of the year, I could only hope he'd let me apologise and hear me out.

It had taken barely two minutes for reality to hit me square in the face after I'd reacted the way I had. Two short minutes for me to recognise I'd quite possibly screwed up the best thing I'd ever had.

Because Riley was it. The one. And my knee-jerk panic was responsible for ruining that. My brain unravelling and immediately landing on James and the memory of receiving the call from the hospital was all it took for me to destroy us—the incredible relationship I had with Riley.

Fear had pulsed a heavy beat in my heart. First thinking of James, then imagining my life without Riley in it. It was then the truth had hit me: I loved him.

Perhaps it was selfish of me to be hanging around, desperate for him to hear me out, my confession, hell, my declaration. But I couldn't give up.

The sound of an engine had my heart beating quicker and me sitting up higher in my seat. Disappointment slammed into me. It wasn't him.

Turning my focus to my phone, I hit his contact again. The call rang out until it flipped to his voice-mail. I'd already left one, apologising, calling myself a dick, and begging him to let me see him. I'd said as much in frantic text messages too.

Throwing my phone on the passenger seat, I sat in contemplative silence. It was impossible to not overthink the moment, go over what I should have done and said. How I should have responded.

It was thirty minutes until another car appeared. This time, I jumped out of my truck immediately, shoved my keys in my pocket, and ignored how my heart sank at the look on his face as he passed me by and pulled up onto his small driveway.

Once out of his car, Riley didn't even glance in my direction, a reaction I deserved. But I had to try.

"I'm so sorry," I called out, stepping closer and pausing at the back of his car. His key was already in the lock, but he hesitated at my words. Hope slammed into me, thick and fast. "I reacted... so fucking badly. And there's no excuse."

He angled towards me at that, the creases around his eyes tight, hurt clear in every line. "I can't talk to you right now."

I nodded and hesitated, so desperate for him to hear me out, but pushing would mean I wasn't listening to a thing he was saying. Swallowing hard and forcing back the need to forge ahead, I settled on "Can we perhaps talk tomorrow?" Intensity filled my request, sorrow and determination to make this right thrumming deep inside.

His gaze roamed over my face, darting from my eyes to my mouth before he glanced down, a heavy sigh escaping. The sound tore at me. I was the reason for the hurt radiating off him. I hesitated for the first time, wondering whether or not he was better off without me and my hang-ups. I'd thrown everything at him so unexpectedly, wounded him so severely, and possibly done irrevocable damage to any future we had together.

But I loved him with an intensity that burned brightly. The words sat on my tongue, and singed, eager to be released. For me to throw an "I love you" at him now, though, was beyond wrong, so instead, I painfully swallowed the words and waited, silently pleading Riley would give me a chance I didn't deserve.

After a few tense moments, he nodded. "Does eleven give you enough time to get things done on the property?"

My heart lurched. This man was too good for me. Kind, understanding, and thoughtful, Riley deserved nothing but honesty and goodness. I vowed to myself as I nodded and said, "Absolutely. I'll be here. Thank you," that starting tomorrow, there'd be no holding back.

Holding tightly to the glimmer of hope he offered, I headed back to my ute, casting him one final look before I pulled away. Riley's gaze was on my vehicle, and I prayed to every deity I could think of that his unwillingness to look away was a good sign.

Within a couple of hours, I was back home and doing a piss-poor job of keeping myself busy while dodging Pops's disappointed looks.

When I'd shown up without Riley, he'd known instantly something was wrong. Perhaps from my inability to maintain eye contact with him for long, he'd soon figured out I was the dipshit responsible for the ache in my heart and the empty seat at the dining table.

"And you walked away?" He shook his head, displeasure evident in his tone as well as the steely look he sent my way. "Twice." A heavy sigh escaped him. "Shit, son, what the hell were you thinking? It was bad enough you walked away at the beach, but then you did so at the house too."

"What?" I said a little defensively, "I could hardly force him to talk to me, especially when he asked me to leave."

"He actually said that?"

Dipping my brows low, I considered the tense moments in front of his house. "Well, not exactly no. But he said he didn't want to talk to me and agreed to talk to me tomorrow."

Pops huffed out a humourless breath. "If he's got any sense, he'll not be home or change his mind."

Panic punched hard against my chest. "Shit, you think?"

He shrugged. "Person I was dating walked away from me without a fight, I would. Can't be that keen to make amends."

"Shit, Pops, but he's not you. I was listening and being respectful."

"That what you were doing?"

Exhaustion edged into my vision, the distress of today, the screw-up riding me hard. "Yes."

Hard eyes stared back at me, and Pops quirked his brow high. "You sure about that? You weren't just slightly relieved to avoid a difficult conversation?"

"No," I said immediately, though his words burrowed into my head, implanting a seed of doubt. Was that what I'd been doing? Admittedly, a part of me hoped a good night's sleep would give us both a clearer head, but what if Pops was right, and with a clear head, all it did was give Riley more time to recognise I wasn't worth it?

My heart galloped in my chest, pounding so hard it stuttered my breathing.

"Shit." I shot up out of my chair and made a beeline

for the side table. Swiping my keys and my phone, I focused on trying to get my heart rate down. I rubbed at my chest, my heart legit aching. "I've gotta go."

"And there it is. About bloody time. Don't be coming back till you sort everything out. Grovel on your knees if you have to. It always worked for your grandma when I was in the doghouse. That and a good rogering."

I blanched, wanting to pour bleach into my eyes at the image of that. It had the desired effect—calming my heartbeat and slowing my breathing. Pops was smiling way too big, considering the situation. I hesitated. "What if—"

"Stop being a whinging wuss and get your arse into action."

I nodded and grasped my keys tightly in my hand.

"You love the boy, right?"

My bobbing head was immediate. "Yeah."

"No more messing around then, son. Go."

My smile was tentative, but a renewed sense of purpose thrummed a new beat. I could only hope Riley gave me a chance, deserving or not. I was aware I was discounting his wishes by showing up unannounced. While I didn't want to ruin my chances for good or hurt Riley any more than I already had, the pain slashing deep inside when I thought of him home and vulnerable was too much to bear.

I hesitated before opening my car door. I was being a selfish prick by ignoring his request.

But, fuck, I didn't think I could rest until I checked with my own eyes that he was okay. That he was safe.

I huffed out a breath and leaned against the closed door. Riley deserved my respect and understanding, and so much more. Me rocking up at his house unannounced would be going completely against that. Decision made, I headed back inside, each step painful and forced.

I needed to do this on his terms. It was the only way.

Chapter Fifteen

RILEY

It was times like these, even in the brightness of a brand-new day, when I considered breaking the promise I'd made to myself all those years ago. A beer, or something a little harder, would have helped me right about now. Aiden was due anytime soon and my nerves rode me. There was no chance of me having a beer though. I'd been dependent on alcohol once, in those long, painful months after the accident until I'd tried to commit suicide.

Never again.

It had been when my wrists were wrapped in bandages and after the first session with the hospital psychologist, the harsh face of reality had hit me.

I'd almost died. It was a miracle I hadn't. And what would my sister have thought about that?

It was at that point with the no-bullshit doctor that I knew deep in my very being I had to stop the spiral. After the accident, alcohol had become my companion. Every sip I took I'd hated, knowing that drinking had been the reason my sister had been on the road in the first place. It wasn't until after I survived and during countless hours of therapy, I finally believed the accident wasn't my fault. And one of the promises I made to myself during my sessions was to never touch a drop of alcohol again.

Now, sitting on my sofa in front of a brain-numbing show, instead of vodka, I wrapped my palms around a mug of tea.

Hanging out with Pete last night had helped for a little while. My mind had calmed enough to get myself home safely so I could wallow. What I hadn't accounted for was Aiden waiting for me.

I hated myself for the thrill and warmth that immediately bloomed to life when I saw him. He'd hurt me, bad. I scoffed just thinking about it. "Bad" was a massive understatement. Yet still, I'd agreed to meet with him, even been considerate enough to consider what time he could come around safely without it interfering with his chores.

I exhaled heavily. Perhaps I was a sucker for punishment. One of my other promises flickered to life in my mind, another I'd made all those years ago.

Anger was a brutal, dangerous emotion. My own had resulted in the car crash, my sister's injuries, and my own suicide attempt. So promising myself to work my arse off at expelling anger from my heart was as natural as it was challenging. A lot of therapy had helped me reach this point.

There were a lot of dickheads in the world, so stepping away or trying to rationalise my feelings to simply let it go was hard work at times. In many ways, it was why I led such a simple, quiet life. It was easier to protect my heart by keeping myself cut off from the world.

And then Aiden happened.

While everything had been so easy and right between us, it meant my heart opened, became vulnerable, and look where that got me.

I sipped my tea, allowing its sweetness to do its job, and sighed happily.

Aiden's face though—

I closed my eyes, looking at the devastation in the depth of his eyes when he'd stood outside my home. His "sorry" had held urgency, desperation for me to believe him. The thing was, I did believe him. The man had no reason to deceive me with empty apologies. But then there was his reaction at the beach. It had been raw, fierce, and real. His distress, horror, hell, maybe even disgust had been palpable.

How could I ever forget or forgive that?

I finished off my drink and switched off the TV. Sitting and overthinking did me no good.

I stood and headed to the kitchen to rinse my mug. The knock on the door had me jumping and dropping the ceramic in the sink. It fell with a clatter. I glanced at it, expecting to see it in pieces. It wasn't—surprising after the hit it had taken. Even the most fragile of things could bounce back.

Exhaling heavily, I headed to the door. A quick glance at the time told me Aiden was early, as I had no doubt who it was. My heart jumped into my throat, not completely prepared to see him yet. A spark lit in my chest, and I struggled to catch hold of a single emotion. I took a breath and opened the door. Aiden stood there, eyes wide, cheeks red, and his Adam's apple bobbing when he saw me.

"I'm early, I know. Is that okay?" The words raced out of him on a quiet, nervous breath. "I know you said eleven, but I struggled to wait any longer. Please just let me know you're okay. I can then go and grab a coffee or something if you want me to. Come back at eleven?"

My gut clenched. Aiden may be trying to make things right, but the hurt festered inside my chest, bitter and acrid. "I'm hurt, but okay."

He nodded and seemed to hesitate. I exhaled and indicated with raised brows that he could say more.

"I messed up. I'm so sorry, Riley." A loud swallow followed his words. "I need to tell you about James," he said in another rushed breath, perhaps seeing my hesitation. It had the desired effect. What did his old boyfriend have to do with this? My brows dipped low, but before I could speak, he added, "About how he died."

And there it was, the crux of it all. Nausea swirled in my stomach. My heart lurched at both the pain floating between us and the rawness of every-thing. Already I had a good idea of what he was going to say, but all being said, assumptions were not going to help this situation. They certainly wouldn't help heal the fractures in my heart, so with a small bob of my head, I stepped back, holding the door open for Aiden.

"Come on in. Tea?"

His relief was immediate, evident in the shine and lightness in his eyes and the ease in his shoul-ders. Though I'd hear him out, the weight in my stomach refused to move. While I had no idea how our conversation would end, giving him a chance to say his peace I could do.

With the tea steaming in the mugs, we sat on the sofa at either end, angled into each other. It felt too casual, too much considering the ripple of tension between us. Yet even with the metre or so between us, it felt unnatural Aiden being so far away and not in my arms. I exhaled heavily, trying to keep on top of my confusing emotions. Was it only yesterday I'd greeted him with a kiss I'd felt in every nerve ending and with the three words so eager to escape on my tongue?

Already it felt like a lifetime ago.

When he took a sip of tea, his eyes connected with mine. I tensed, waiting for him to begin. Aiden didn't keep me waiting long before he started.

"I already told you how James and I were having a few problems when he'd died." He had, on one of the nights when we shared stories about our pasts. "I know I hinted that the issues ran deeper. James had paranoid schizophrenia. He went undiagnosed for years, well before we met. When we were together, he was treated for bipolar disorder. He was on mood stabilisers, and they helped for a while... until they didn't. He pulled away, withdrew, and by that point, life was hard... for both of us." Aiden's gaze remained intensely focused on me as he spoke. Hurt and pain filtered through his voice with every syllable, though, and while I still expected I knew what was coming, I waited, listening intently, my own pain drifting to the surface. But this time it was for him, and for James.

"Three times he'd had failed suicide attempts." Aiden shook his head, his eyes tearing. "I was so angry, heartbroken that he could do that to me. By the time the fourth attempt came, this one doing the job, I finally understood that his suicide wasn't about me at all. And it wasn't him, it was his illness. Early on, I wondered if I'd left him, maybe he would have found the help that he needed, maybe I was dragging him down even more. I've had some counselling, but honestly, after how I reacted yesterday —" He paused and shook his head. "Maybe I'm not as over what happened after all."

Tears sprung in his eyes, and the desire to reach out and comfort him bubbled to inside me. But I needed to hear it all, didn't want him to stop.

"The week it happened, we were having a really good week." He scoffed without a trace of humour. "They were so rare that when I left him that morning to head out for a muster, I actually wondered if it was the calm before the storm. There was a ball in the pit of my stomach, but I was too damn terrified to rock the boat. He'd been doing so well for a few weeks, even though he wasn't being great on his meds, and we'd actually laughed and joked that morning. As soon as I stepped foot into the house, I felt it like a punch to the gut that something wasn't right."

I closed my eyes as he spoke, a lone tear escaping and trickling down my cheek. "You found him?" The question broke free unbidden. I opened my eyes to see Aiden nod, his lips pulled in between his teeth.

"Yeah. Tried CPR, but it was no good, and the hospital was over an hour away."

"I'm so sorry you had to go through that." My hand found his, no longer able to stop myself from offering him comfort.

"It was the worst day of my life, but it's only recently I've come to terms with my own pain and truly thought about just how alone and terrified James must have been. For his pain to overshadow our smiles and laughter to such an extent..." He gulped hard, the tears in his eyes finally spilling. "Fuck, I can't even imagine. And I'm so fucking sorry. I forgot that, when I saw your tattoo, saw your wrists, I just thought about me rather than thinking about you and how fucking brave you are to be here. You're so strong, so much stronger than I could ever be."

Every trace of my anger escaped in a huff of breath as I moved over and wrapped him in my arms. His grip was fierce, unyielding as he pressed his face to my neck and heaved a sob that latched on to my heart and squeezed tight.

"You really hurt me," I whispered. "You can't hurt me like that." Fresh tears sprung to my eyes as I spoke, needing him to hear and feel every word. I understood his pain, but mine was just as real.

"I won't." Aiden pulled away and clasped my face between his two strong hands. "I promise I will never hurt you like that again. You matter to me. Mean everything."

I closed my eyes at his words, loving this man so damn much. "Don't break my heart again." My words were quiet, laced with pain and uncertainty, though I felt bold for speaking the truth.

Aiden's watery gaze flicked between mine and my mouth and back again. He took a shuddering breath, his thumb brushing over my bottom lip. "I promise I won't."

"And I really think maybe it would be a good idea for you to get some support, talk through some more what happened with James and how it's impacted on your everyday life. You're still so angry."

He nodded. "You're right. I know rationally the right way I should react, how I should feel. I even know that James isn't to blame, but then a spark of anger just pops out of nowhere, and I know that's not fair on me, and it's definitely not fair on you. I promise to arrange something."

A swell of emotion clogged my throat, catching my words. Unable to speak, I nodded.

"If you trust me with your heart again, I'll look after it, you, and what we have. I love you too much to screw this up again."

My breath caught at his words, my heart finally beating a tempo no longer shrouded in desperation and loss. "Just kiss me," I said.

His mouth was on mine in an instant.

Despite the suddenness of his movement, his mouth pressed gently against mine.

I'd expected urgency, desperation, but it was so much more. When Aiden captured my mouth and trailed his tongue over my salt-soaked lips, it was soft, not quite tentative. The kisses he trailed down my neck and back up again before dotting them on my mouth were almost reverent in the tenderness.

I savoured every single one, my heart bruised

and struggling to calm after the hurt that had splintered it. But Aiden's gentle caresses, his whispered words of love began to soothe my soul.

He sucked gently on my bottom lip before pulling away, leaving me breathless. When our eyes connected, my heart stuttered at the intensity directed my way.

"I hope you'll find a way to forgive me." The whispered words pressed against my skin. Aiden didn't wait for an answer, saying, "I know it'll take time, but I want you, want us to work."

Hope and desperation, so wildly opposite, zipped in the space between us. I snatched at the former, wanting the same as him, wanting his heart to be mine always. Only together could we work through this, could I fully forgive him, which I was already so close to doing after he'd told me about James. And there was trust.

"Can I trust you with my heart?" I asked. My words were quiet and uncertain.

He didn't answer immediately, didn't rush in with platitudes and more apologies. Instead, his intense stare seemed to penetrate my soul as he seemed to absorb every single nuance. Reaching out for my hand, he held it, clasping my large hand in his. "Yes. I want to prove that to you every single day we're together, always if you'll let me."

Emotion rolled over me like a tidal wave, exhaustion churning and forcing me to take a deep, shuddering breath. My shoulders sagged, and I smiled.

A spark of wonder fired in my brain. My smile was real, genuine despite that just a few hours ago, in the pits of melancholy, I couldn't even dream of a time I would do so again.

"Okay." I nodded, my mouth still curving upwards.

A tentative smile settled on his lips. With flushed cheeks and bright eyes directed my way, I knew my simple one-word response had made its mark.

"But all I want to do right now is crash. I'm wiped." My sleep had been nothing short of abysmal. It wasn't even midday, but I needed to rest so I could function.

"Oh, okay. Do you want me to go?"

There wasn't a chance I'd be letting him leave. I needed him in my arms, in my bed. The thought of heading back to his was too much; the exhaustion biting at my heels wouldn't allow it.

"You've got your chores," I acknowledged.

Aiden shook his head, surprising me. "Jerry's covering for me. I'd like to stay, if that's okay? I'll call him later to see if he's okay to step in tomorrow morning too."

"Yeah, I'd like that."

The new tension between us felt strange. Not quite wrong, but with our nerves on edge and emotion still clinging to the air, it was to be expected. And when we stood, his hand in mine as we headed to my bedroom, I figured it would take some time to find the ease and comfort we once had. But just maybe we'd be the stronger for it.

Chapter Sixteen

THE WEEK THAT FOLLOWED MY EPIC FAILURE OF BEING the supportive, understanding boyfriend was a bit of a blur. With our relationship still tender, I wanted to up my game and reassure Riley that while I'd been a prize fool, he could trust me and I was worth it.

On Monday, I'd met Riley in his work's car park, surprising him. My extra early start that morning was worth it, if only to see the pleasure he wasn't good at concealing on his face. We walked on the beach that evening before heading back to his for dinner. I'd offered to take us out, but Riley, being the man he was, could see through my exhaustion something fierce so insisted we headed to his.

I'd left that night far too late for the long journey

home, but the sweet smile and not-so-chaste kiss before I buckled into my ute was totally worth it.

On Tuesday, we met in Gympie directly after his work, saving me the added drive. We headed to the movies and made out like a couple of teenagers in the half-empty cinema. I couldn't remember the last time I'd necked in the movie theatre. Honestly, I was grateful for it as, by far, getting all hot and bothered and not being able to do a thing about it was kinda sexy and cemented a new favourite memory for me.

By the time Wednesday came around, I'd been chewing at the bit as I waited for him to arrive. Pops had made a big fuss of him and surprised both Riley and me by hauling him into a hug. Since Pops was the least tactile guy I knew and rarely warmed to people, that night, I'd curled around Riley feeling additionally sappy as I'd taken him with my mouth, finishing off with my hand as I whispered sweet nothings to him.

It played on my mind that he hadn't said those three words back, but I wasn't arsehole enough to think he owed me them or I deserved them. Plus, just because I'd told him how I felt didn't mean he was obligated to feel the same or even tell me if he did.

But hell, I hoped he did.

Thursday, we spent two hours on a video call, which completely surprised the hell out of me. Who the heck knew I could talk for so long on the phone, but even as we'd said goodbye, both of us knackered, our eyes rolling, I'd been reluctant to let him go. Phones were not my thing at all. The truth was, I kinda resented the device, even though I knew how practical and important it was. But last night, nobody would have guessed that by the way I practically cradled it in my hands, enjoying us shooting the shit about nothing and everything.

The late afternoon sky was still bathed in sunlight as I looked to the horizon. My gaze was on the plume of dust in the distance, my heart already tripping over itself. In two minutes, my mouth would be on his.

In no time at all, I opened the car door. Riley's face was tipped up in my direction, a broad smile on his face. "Hey, you," he said.

I grinned back and leaned into him before he had the opportunity to unclip his seat belt. "Hey," I greeted before I brushed my mouth against his. When he sighed into the kiss, my tripping heart did a somersault. "Good journey?" I asked as I pulled back, giving him room to step out.

"Yeah. No dramas. Can you grab Timmy's gift off the back seat while I grab my bag?"

My chest tightened that he'd bought Timmy a present for his birthday. "Absolutely."

We gathered his things and went into the main house. Pops was around at our neighbour Bob's house, an old farmer he enjoyed chewing the fat with, so we were alone for a couple of hours.

"You all done for the day?" he asked as I led him to my bedroom after he'd placed Timmy's wrapped gift on the kitchen table.

"Yeah. Wasn't sure if you wanted some fresh air, go for a walk or something. I know you're missing your walk."

"Sounds good."

Riley changed his clothes while I put the casserole in the oven on low to warm up, courtesy of Pops who was surprisingly good at cooking. He returned to the kitchen, a tentative smile on his face and saying, "Smells good."

"All down to Pops." I tilted my head, wondering if something was wrong. "You okay?"

There was a small hesitation, a purse of his lips before he spoke. "Can we actually talk?"

Fear struck me fast and fierce at those words.

"We can do so as we're walking." If he noticed my worry, he didn't say a thing, but taking my hand in his made it easier to shake my concern.

For a few painful minutes, we walked in silence. The cicadas were beginning to chant, welcoming dusk in, and a few weaning calves hollered in the distance. While I was aware of the sounds, I was more aware of my heart's heavy pounding in my ears, the crunch of the dry grass under my boots.

"This week you've been amazing," he said, his voice and the words themselves startling me. "But"—I flinched at that one word, too fucking sensitive for my own good after the shitshow of last weekend—"we can't keep going on like this."

I stopped short. My feet rooted to the spot. While my mind was buzzing with possibilities, I forced myself to take a calming breath, needing clarification. I moved my thumb, my skin brushing his, the contact reminding me we were still connected. "What do you mean?" I peered across at him as he moved, grip remaining in mine, to stand before me. His gaze softened, and he reached across, sweeping his finger between my brows, trying to ease the frown settled there. "Not whatever you may be thinking," he said, his gaze soft and his smile warm.

The exhale that escaped my lungs didn't go unnoticed, but I didn't have it in me to be embarrassed. After last weekend, I'd committed to both of us to aim for full disclosure. That meant no holding back.

"So, this week you've been amazing," he repeated, his smile still in place. "And I love seeing you, spending as much time as possible with you, but not when it brings you to your knees with how bolloxed you are."

I made to answer, my mouth opening to shut him down and let him know I didn't mind. The squeeze of his hand stopped me.

"What I'm saying is I know you're sorry, and I know that things have seemed a bit... I don't know, strained isn't the right word, but it's like you're walking on eggshells." Heat hit my cheeks at his accurate description. "You fucked up, but I understand why and I believe you when you say you'll do your best to never do so again. But let's just..." He seemed to be searching for a word.

"Be?" I asked, earning me a nod and a broader smile.

"Yeah. What we have is amazing. We'll get to the point naturally when we see each other every day, and it'll be because we've figured out the next step and are living together."

This time, it was Riley's cheeks that heated. My stomach somersaulted, looking at the man before me and listening to his quietly confident words. He seemed so different on the surface, transformed almost from the man I met a few months back on that first hike. But I knew so much better. This strength that he displayed right now, and time and time again since we'd been dating, was unassuming. That didn't undermine his resolve or fire.

The pounding of my heart kicked up. Worry was no longer the driving factor, though. Instead, Riley's words sparked my absolute desire for the future he envisioned for us to come true.

"Okay," I said, my lips curved upwards. "I want that too, more than anything."

"Yeah?"

"Absolutely. I love you, Riley. That future... it's what I want too."

Riley's large arms looped around me and hauled me close so I was wrapped up, pressed against soft skin and flesh and the perfect strength that was all Riley. "I love you too." The words brushed against my ear. I caught my breath, squeezing tighter before pulling away. I couldn't have eased the shit-eating grin on my face if I'd have tried. Not that I wanted to. Riley deserved every emotion and fragment of joy I could share with him.

"Yeah?" I said for the second time, not trusting myself to articulate myself better.

"Oh yeah." He paired the words with light laughter and bobbing brows before tugging me back and catching my mouth with his. Heat licked at me on the ferocity of the need pulsing between us.

Riley had been absolutely right. I'd been holding back, scared about pushing my luck or stepping on his toes.

Energy raced through my veins, freeing me entirely as I took what I needed while pouring all the love and desire I had for the man in my arms into our kiss.

"How long till your pops gets back?" he asked after easing back, panting slightly.

"We've got enough time if we head back now rather than finish our walk."

"Sounds like a plan."

Together, we raced to the house, my hand already on the front of his jeans and undoing his button and zip.

By the time we stumbled into my bedroom, we were laughing, our jeans around our ankles and trying desperately to kick them off while pulling our shirts off. Like this, with laughter, lightness, and a whole lot of heat in our love, I had a feeling we'd need to be figuring out just how we wanted to organise our future sooner rather than later.

Chapter Seventeen

RILEY

I traced my tattoo with my forefinger, thinking about how far I'd come and how much had changed.

"Hey."

Aiden's voice pulled my attention to the open doorway to his en suite. His gaze flicked to my wrist, and he smiled, a flicker of emotion coming to life in his eyes. Just a week ago, I would have hidden and been mortified for him seeing me do such a thing. Honestly, when I thought about my tattoo and my past, an avalanche of emotions still tended to derail me.

A little shame, a little guilt, a little pride; it remained confusing, especially considering my sister's health. But Aiden's gaze, which flicked to me as he stepped towards his bed where I was lounging, dragged out the delicious feeling of hope.

He sat and lifted my wrist, pressing a kiss on the inked skin. The tender gesture sparked a flicker of awareness in me. Speaking softly, he all but breathed the words "I've decided this punctuation mark right here needs attention every single day."

I quirked my brow at that.

His gaze skated over my face, though he didn't comment on my drawn brows. "This," he said, dotting another soft kiss against the mark, "right here shows me you love yourself."

I swallowed hard at his words and smiled faintly.

"And because you love yourself, it means you were able to open up your heart to let me in there too. Love me."

Unable to resist touching him, I sat and cupped his cheek. "Thank you."

A quick bob of his head followed before he stood a little abruptly. "Stay where you are." His smile quirked to the one side slightly, a nervous tell I'd come to notice. Aiden headed to his set of drawers and rifled through.

"You know, there's still plenty of lube and condoms in this special drawer right here," I said a little quickly, trying to shake the nerves settling in me. It got me a look, a quirked brow, and a laugh.

"That there is." He wriggled his brows, helping ease the tension in my shoulders. "Speaking of, I was hoping we could talk about getting tested at some point."

My eyes shot wide, and heat flashed in my body at the thought of being rid of the latex. "Oh, wow, are you looking for forms or something?"

His laughter was loud, lighting up his face beautifully. I couldn't help the small sigh that escaped. Aiden had this whole rugged, country thing going on, so he was always sexy. Add his incredible laugh, and I'd happily lie back and watch and listen to him all damn day and night.

"No." He shook his head. "I got side-tracked, but give it some thought. We can talk about it some—"

"No." The word rushed out. "I'd like that a lot," I admitted. "Perhaps we can make an appointment together."

The way pink crawled up his neck had me shifting on the bed, my cock growing despite us not having long blown each other's minds.

"We can do that." Gaze back on the drawer, he continued to search, finally pulling free a small paper bag. When he returned his attention to me, his cheeks were still flushed, and the nervousness from a few moments ago was back.

Making his way back to me, he didn't allow his gaze to wander. It remained intent, focused. My eyes dipped to the bag as he sat before meeting his.

His tongue flicked out, the slightest wipe of his dry bottom lip, and he exhaled, a tentative smirk on his lips. "I bought you this." He handed over the small bag, and I took it off him with raised brows.

"Should I be nervous? You're looking all kinds of intense there."

A huff of low laughter was his response before he said, "No, but I also want to explain when you open it."

"Okay."

I opened the bag and peered inside, my eyes widening and my heart immediately tripping over itself. The leather was smooth and cool in my fingers, and I stroked the soft woven bands as I pulled the gift out. A leather band with a small silver rectangle wedged in the middle sat in my palm.

While it was different from the one I lost, I understood the sentiment.

When I glanced up, those intense eyes of his were zeroed in on me and my reaction. "I know it can never replace Tanya's, and I also don't want you to think you have to hide your wrists or your tattoo, but I wanted to give it to you as a reminder of me and everything we have together."

The whole time he spoke, I bit the inside of my cheeks. The past week had been a constant whirlwind of emotions—good and bad—and tears—happy and sad. I'd hoped to be over the tidal wave, exhausted of dealing with the heaviness of it all. But then Aiden had to go and do something so bloody sweet that I struggled to contain it all.

"It's beautiful." I examined the leather band more carefully, using the time to calm my heart that was fit to burst. The brushed silver was a little different and quirky. It'd look nice against my skin. I flicked it over. My breath caught, and it was no good.

"Bloody hell." I sniffed and shook my head, my watery eyes connecting with his. "Stop with all of this emotional shit already." My words came out as a garbled laugh, emotion riding me high. I glanced down again and trailed the small inscription on the underside of the silver.

For all our tomorrows.

Between the similar words from the quote I'd shared with him and our own talks of our future, it wasn't hard to see where his inspiration had come from. That he'd done something so thoughtful all but blew my mind. And my heart was fit to burst… it was too late to keep it whole. While I'd already told Aiden I loved him, this moment right here brought a new level of love that I could never have prepared for, didn't even know existed.

"Is it okay?"

His quietly spoken words filtered through my whole heart-eruption thing I had going on. "I love it," I managed to say before reaching out to him and tugging none too lightly in my direction, encouraging him to press his body against mine.

He landed with an *oomph* and a smile, his eyes wide and bright. "You really love it?"

I bobbed my head, despite the awkwardness against the pillow. "It's perfect. Thank you." I followed up with a kiss and shuffled to open my legs, encouraging him between them.

Once settled, he caressed my cheek with his rough palm and leaned into it. I nuzzled against it and shifted my hips, making it absolutely clear with my hard-on I was ready to thank him in another way too.

He grinned, his hand moving to my briefs. Fingers hooking under the elastic, he—

"You've had more than enough time to be catching up and screwing, boys. Get your arses outta that hovel so you can come and keep an old man company."

His pops's voice was loud and clear and had me laughing and Aiden groaning against my neck, hand frozen in place.

"We could pretend we're not here, and we're out in the shed or something."

I snorted. "As if he'll buy that. Give it more than five minutes and he'll be banging on the door." And I didn't even mind. Okay, perhaps I cared a bit, as my cock was hard and I had all of these feelings still racing around, but it was his pops, and the man was growing on me.

"Five minutes?" Bouncing brows followed his words.

"Wow. You're saying that in a way that you think it should tempt me?" I teased, settling into the ease between us, enjoying how it helped to calm my soul.

He squinted at me. "Now four minutes and forty seconds, and I reckon I can have you shooting your load."

Interest spiked inside me, right alongside my amusement. "Down your throat?" I challenged.

Laughter burst out of me, loud and freeing, when he shifted off me so fast and tugged my briefs down so damn quickly he yanked me a good foot down the bed.

"Time me!" Nothing but love shone in his eyes right before he licked under my cock and proceeded to prove that all he needed was three minutes and twenty-seven seconds.

AIDEN

NERVES RADIATED OFF THE MAN AT MY SIDE. ALL I could do was squeeze Riley's hand and offer him another smile of encouragement.

For months we'd planned this visit, ten of them to be exact, almost immediately after that disastrous moment I'd almost ruined the best thing I'd ever had.

Three weeks after that awful day at the beach, we'd escaped for two nights away in Airlie Beach, chasing the space to talk and reconcile thoroughly. It was over that weekend that Riley held my hand when I filled in the enquiry form for suicide grief counselling and he opened up to me about his attempted suicide.

The weekend had been cathartic, and what we'd both needed to find our footing.

For the past eight months, the sessions had enabled me to find true peace and acceptance while ensuring I could be my best self to support Riley and all he had been through.

His situation was completely different to that of James, whose battle with mental illness had ended too soon. I know that now, completely. The emotional hell leading to Riley's struggle, his complete isolation, his guilt, how he'd been abandoned had built to a tsunami of loss and devastation he'd struggled to escape from. But he had. Miraculously so, and well before I was lucky enough to call him mine.

But there was this last thing he needed to do. Being here for him, and Riley knowing with 100 percent certainty that I loved him and had his back, I hoped was all the reassurance this man of mine needed to step through the automatic doors to the care home facility.

"What if they don't let me see her?" A tremor latched on to Riley's words.

"That's not going to happen. You called ahead, you double-checked visitation rights, and you know there's nothing in Tanya's paperwork stipulating you don't have access to her for a visit." He'd been surprised as hell by that too. His parents in their shittiness had restricted phone calls between Riley and his sister. But since the man of mine had long since won the long-term staff over—they gave small phone updates while ensuring they didn't overstep the rules by allowing Riley to speak to Tanya, they'd poured through the contract with his parents and came back triumphant.

Phone and video calls were restricted. Physical visits were not mentioned once.

"You're right. Okay." Riley pressed his lips together and stared at the closed doors. I remained silent at his side, wishing I could help him through this so much more. "I'm nervous as hell." The words escaped as a whisper.

Unable to hold back any longer, I tugged him towards a wooden bench just off to the right and got him to sit beside me. He dropped down with a heavy sigh, the sound hurting my heart with the uncertainty and exhaustion I heard crystal clear.

Angling towards him, I took hold of his hand. "Remind me what today is about." Quiet encouragement filled my words. I wanted to remind him of the countless conversations we'd had, not only between the two of us, but the few times he'd joined me for grief counselling sessions.

Riley lifted his gaze, his eyes softening at contact. Before he spoke, he released a long breath, his whole body all but deflating before me as some of the tension seemed to melt away from his no-longer rigid shoulders. "I want to see her face. I need to see her chest rise and fall. Her room... I want to make sure it's not filled with old lady stuff by Mum, as she'd absolutely hate that."

I smiled softly at his words, and his lips lifted a little despite the new shine in his eyes. "What else?"

"I want to hold her hand so she knows I haven't forgotten her, and there's a heap of crappy jokes I've memorised that are so bad that she really needs to hear them. She was the queen of crap jokes." He released a watery chuckle. "I need to tell her I love her."

I nodded, swallowing hard. I couldn't hide the impact of his words though. With my heart in my throat, I reached out and caught him up in a hug. I held him tightly, squeezing so he'd feel just how much he was cared for, loved.

"Let's go do this then. I need to meet the woman who hit Mute on scary movies and did voiceovers to stop you pissing your pants in fear."

Riley burst out laughing and wiped his eyes. "She was just as scared."

"Uh-huh, but it was super sweet all the same."

He bobbed his head. "It was, but she wasn't always sweet." He quirked a brow.

I grinned, already thinking of one of the many stories he'd told me about. "And you still can't eat beef jerky?"

Narrowed eyes glared back at me.

"What?" I said, laughing. "Easy enough to be tricked on that one." When he'd told me how his sister shared her "jerky" with him for years, only to be told later that the jerky was actually dog treats, I may have snorted too damn hard.

"Even the smell of the things makes me want to gag." Riley shuddered.

Our laughter filtered away and we slipped into silence. When he was ready, he'd let me know. Meanwhile, I took in the place. The care home was close to a large park we'd walked past to get here. Riley had said that the home took regular trips out, and I liked to think residents were out as often as busy schedules allowed. I couldn't imagine being stuck indoors.

My pops told stories of me wearing boots, usually his, and clomping around the yards from the moment I could walk. My folks had had to drag me back inside kicking and screaming as he told it. Apparently on more than one occasion someone would find me covered in mozzie bites at five in the morning as I'd snuck outside to sleep under the stars.

"Okay."

Riley's steady voice drew my attention. A tentative smile lifted his lips and he stood. I followed suit and reached out, taking his hand in mine.

Silently, we headed towards the automatic doors. This time, they opened once we reached the sensor and we stepped in. The reception was pleasant, painted yellow. A collection of artwork scattered the walls, the nameplates indicating they were work from the residents.

A middle-aged woman with a warm smile greeted us. "Morning. You here to visit someone?"

Riley bobbed his head and expelled a breath. "Yeah, I'm Riley. I'm here to see my sister, Tanya."

The woman's eyes widened in recognition, and her smile grew. "Riley, it's so wonderful to put a face to the voice. I'm Carrie."

There was a subtle shift in Riley's body language, and I peered to my side to look at him. Relief swept over him thick and fast—the lines between his brows smoothed out, his shoulders relaxed, and a smile curved his lips.

"Carrie, hey, you too. I can't thank you enough for, well... everything."

Her smile softened and she reached out and squeezed Riley's forearm. "You're welcome. Right, I imagine you're keen to visit your sister." At Riley's nod, she indicated towards the paperwork on the desk. "Just get all these filled in for me, then I'll get the both of you visitor badges and you'll be all set. Tanya's having a great morning so far. I know she'll be happy to see you."

"Thanks." I reached out and took the paperwork and started filling everything in. Before coming, we'd already discussed expectations. Tanya had suffered a severe traumatic brain injury, and with a negative reaction to two of her surgeries, she struggled with basic tasks, her speech, and had difficulty getting around. She also had issues with her memories and forming coherent thought. She'd never fully recover from the TBI.

Since it had been so long since Riley had seen his sister, I hoped he was prepared.

With the paperwork complete and our lanyards on, we followed Carrie through a security door and down a wide, bright corridor. More artwork decorated the space. Carrie paused before a painting of reds and greens.

"Your sister's interpretation of a poppy field during one of the art classes," she said, smiling fondly.

Riley's grip on my hand tightened and I stepped closer to him, releasing his hand and placing it on his waist.

"I imagine the talent runs in the family," I offered when Riley remained silent.

Carried chuckled. "Is that right?" She eyed Riley, her gaze softening, no doubt seeing his struggle. "I imagine you prefer painting yourself too, huh?"

Riley looked away from the painting. "Tanya paints herself?"

"She sure does. Finds it highly entertaining too."

Riley's soft laugh helped me breathe a little easier. "That doesn't surprise me. Any chance she could get she'd be painting my face or putting make-up or something on me."

"Make-up, huh? You kept that quiet." I squeezed his waist and Riley peered over to me.

"Not something I plan to repeat, so whatever you're thinking, that'd be a hard no."

God, I loved his smile, loved he wasn't running away from the difficult shit. "I think your eyes would pop with a bit of that liner stuff around them."

He quirked his brow at me and Carrie snorted. "Pop?" Riley said. "Who the hell are you. Pop?"

"What?" I laughed. "I have a sister too."

Warmth filled Riley's gaze when he stared at me, making it hard not to lean into him.

Carrie's voice cut in. "She's in the day room right now. I imagine she'll want to show you her room as well. Just so you know, we'll keep a close eye should any of you need support. Tanya isn't prone to tantrums or acting out, but she can sometimes get frustrated. She doesn't respond well to overly soft tones, you know the ones that can be condescending?"

We both nodded. From the stories of Riley and Tanya's youth, I could only imagine the eye-rolls she could throw anyone's way if someone spoke down to her.

"Sometimes she won't appear to be listening, but there's a good chance she's paying attention to every single word. Physically, she's doing great and is able to walk small distances, but it's hard work for her, so go slow. And everything else, I am confident you'll figure out, but speak to one of the staff if you need anything, okay?"

"Got it." Riley's voice was quiet but steady.

"Come on then." Carrie led us to a large open room, split into various areas by sofas, tables and chairs, and floor cushions.

I glanced around at the residents dotted around the space before focussing on Riley. His breath caught, his gaze intent at the woman sitting by the window, what looked to be cards spread out on the table before her.

"Hey, Tanya. Your visitors have arrived."

It took a few moments for Tanya to show any sign she'd heard Carrie speaking to her, but she did, her eyes wide, bright, and expressive, so much like her brother's.

The sniff at my side broke my heart. But being here was so good for Riley, and I seriously hoped it was good for his sister too. If it wasn't, I would have expected her care worker or whoever supported her would have intervened.

I knew the moment when Tanya registered her brother. A slow smile formed and she picked up one of the cards she'd been pushing around the table. Riley released my hand and I followed his every movement with my eyes.

He was by her side in the next instant, Tanya's gaze tracking him much like mine was. He kneeled before her, reaching and taking both of her hands in his. He spoke quietly, too low for me to hear. Tears tracked his cheeks and my own watery eyes threatened to spill over. Riley then swiped one of Tanya's tears and stroked her cheek before engulfing her in a hug.

A new sniff drew my attention away from Riley and Tanya. Carrie glanced at me with tears streaming. I offered her a kind smile and huffed out a breath, keeping myself in check.

"Why don't you go and get you all a drink from the kitchen area, give them a few moments?"

I bobbed my head and made to follow her.

"Aiden."

Riley's call caught my attention immediately. Question filled his wet eyes, but that was nowhere near what else I saw. Love and happiness shone in their depths, right there alongside the emotion I could only imagine he felt about seeing his sister again.

"Coffee," I offered with a smile. "I'll be back before you know it."

He bobbed his head, a smile joining the movement. "Right back so my sister can start grilling you." He glanced back at his sister and winked at her.

"B-Boy...," she stuttered, hand lifting and tapping

Riley on the cheek. Another mumbled word followed that I didn't quite catch.

"Yes, he is cute," Carrie said from my side, taking me by surprise.

I glanced between the three of them, my heart singing at the delight on Riley's face and the heat in his cheeks.

"I love you, sis, but that cute man over there is all mine." He kissed her cheek and she barked out a laugh. His gaze was then back on me.

The words, his intensity, both combined with the lightness and overflowing emotions, slammed into me. I was absolutely his. Always. And by the end of this visit, I'd make that permanency clear to him, and his sister, offering him the small box that had been burning a hole in my pocket for the past six weeks.

Thank you so much for reading Bounce. I know Riley and Aiden had a few hurdles, but I hope you stuck with them and found the beauty in understanding and forgiveness. Mental illness and depression are challenging topics that needs to be discussed openly and without fear or embarrassment. Should need support, please reach out to your loved ones or health care professionals, also do an internet search for support close to you.

If you're looking for another Australian read, be sure to check out Not Used To Cute. It's sweet and delicious.

I'm curious about your thoughts of Pete. Do you want to see what happens next in his life? Let me know by responding to this survey or dropping me an email. No sign up necessary.

Acknowledgments

This book was cathartic to write. At times, it was also a challenge, so thank you for sticking with it and me. I need to thank my editing team for pushing me, especially Louisa for her thoughtful input and guidance.

My parents deserve a shout out too, not only because they're incredible, but every step of my life, they've supported me, and I've leaned on them so much when struggling through difficult events and my own journey with depression.

Claire at Book Smith is amazing. She understands my process so well, and I wouldn't want to be publishing a book without her involvement.

My wonderful readers at RoMMance with Becca

& Louisa receive an extra thank you. You guys are so supportive. I hope you know how much I appreciate you all.

I live and breathe all things book related. Usually with at least three books being read and two WiPs being written at the same time, life is merrily hectic. I tend to do nothing by halves, so I happily seek the craziness and busyness life offers.

Living on my small property in Queensland with my human family as well as my animal family of cows, chooks, and dogs, I really do appreciate the beauty of the world around me and am a believer that love truly is love.

To check for updates head to my website:
https://beccaseymour.com
You can sign up for my newsletter here:
https://landing.mailerlite.com/webforms/
landing/r9f0i4
Plus, join my Facebook group, which I share with the awesome Louisa Masters here:
https://www.facebook.com/
groups/rommancewithbeccalouisa/

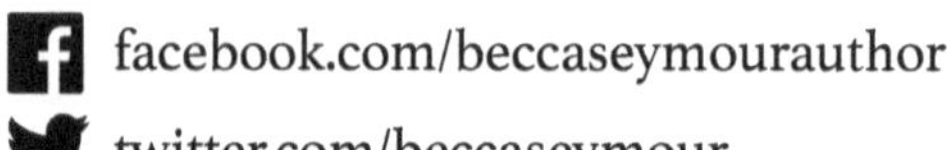

facebook.com/beccaseymourauthor

twitter.com/beccaseymour_

instagram.com/authorbeccaseymour

bookbub.com/authors/becca-seymour